Macauley's Thumb

The

Iowa

Short

Fiction

Award

University of

Iowa Press

Iowa City

Lex
Williford

Macauley's
Thumb

University of Iowa Press, Iowa City 52242

Library of Congress Cataloging-in-Publication Data

Williford, Lex, 1954–

Macauley's thumb / Lex Williford.

p.   cm.—(Iowa short fiction award)

ISBN 0-87745-443-4

I. Title.   II. Series.

PS3573.I45634M3   1994

813'.54—dc20   93-26433

                                                    CIP

98 97 96 95 94 C 5 4 3 2 1

For Lou,

sister and friend

In memory of

Lucile Eastman Akers

FEBRUARY 1896 –

JANUARY 3, 1983

Ruth Snitkin James

OCTOBER 9, 1906 –

JANUARY 2, 1982

Patricia James Davenport

SEPTEMBER 2, 1929 –

APRIL 14, 1992

and

Jennifer Marie Long

MAY 3, 1972 –

APRIL 6, 1991

Contents

ACKNOWLEDGMENTS

Stories in this collection appeared, in slightly
   different form, in the following publications:
   "Pendergast's Daughter" in *Quarterly West* and
   Flash Fiction, "Taking Nonie Home" in the
   Kansas Quarterly, "Fair Day" in the *Virginia
   Quarterly Review*, "A Discussion of Property"
   in *StoryQuarterly*, "Godzilla vs. the Sensitive
   Man" in the *Laurel Review*, "Get Right or Get
   Left" in the *Southern Review*, and "Macauley's
   Thumb" in *Glimmer Train Stories*.
For their support and encouragement, I thank the
   National Endowment of the Arts and Bread Loaf
   Writers' Conference; the Blue Mountain
   Center, the MacDowell Colony, and the
   Corporation of Yaddo; Tess Scogan and Paul
   Parnell; and my parents, Don and Teresa
   Williford.

Macauley's Thumb

Pendergast's Daughter

Leann and I were driving to her father's new A-frame on Lake Nacogdoches, and I was nervous about meeting her folks the first time.

Relax, Leann said. Drink a few Old Mils with Dad, maybe catch a largemouth or two off the dock Saturday. When I got the nerve Sunday, she said, I could spring the news on the old man about wanting to marry his little girl. Then the two of us could get the hell out, head on back to Dallas. Lighten up, she kept saying.

When we got there her kid brother ran to my car, flinging his arms all around. An acre lot across a little inlet was being cleared, flat red clay and loblollies tied with red ribbons. A bulldozer was ramming one of the pines without much luck. Hurry, Leann's brother said.

The lake house was all glass in front so from the gravel drive we could see Mrs. Pendergast inside, slapping the old man's face. Once, twice, then again. She shouted something about him not having any goddamn imagination, about some girl, twenty-six years old, young enough to be his goddamn daughter. He took her flat palms, rigid-faced—just stood there blinking at her. Then his face fell all apart, and he hit her in the sternum with his fist. She staggered back through the open door and up to the balcony rail as he hit her over and over again.

Do something, Leann shouted at me. But I just stood there. I just watched till the old man pushed his wife over the rail.

At the hospital in Lufkin I told Leann, I don't know what the hell happened to me. But then an intern came into the waiting room and said her mom would be all right, just some stitches, some bruised ribs.

Next week I must have left a hundred messages on Leann's answering machine. I'm sorry, they said, you've got to believe me.

I remember we used to shower together every morning I stayed at her garage apartment in University Park. I'd slick her taut brown shoulders with Zest and I'd think, Jesus, this is good.

Taking
Nonie
Home

When they finally arrived at the Hotel Virreynal, Verlin cut the engine and stared out into the cold rain. Like most of the other buildings in Teziutlán, the hotel had slick stone walls, black with mildew and covered with creepers. In the downpour, the place seemed as abandoned to the cloud forests as the Aztec ruins they'd passed driving up into the mountains east of Mexico City.

Verlin leaned across the seat and shook his wife awake. "This is some great idea you had, Liz. Amazing. Really amazing."

Liz squinted. Her red hair stuck up in the back, and there was a sleep crease on her cheek. "You sure this is the place?"

"No, Liz, this is the Mexican presidential palace. Look, I thought you said you checked this place out."

"I did. Nonie wanted to come here and we're here. So why not stay?"

He heard his mother snoring behind him. She lay sprawled in the backseat, her mouth open, her upper plate loose and flapping as she breathed.

"Tell you what," he said, "why don't you and Mama stay? I'll just drop you two off and pick you up later. Say, in a year or two."

Liz ignored him and turned in her seat. "Nonie, honey, we're here."

Verlin helped his mother out of the car, supporting her as she took the hotel steps one at a time. He covered her head with his jacket, but the cold rain came down in sheets from the tiled roof. When they finally got inside the lobby, Liz said, "My God, Verlin, she's soaked."

"You forgot to bring an umbrella," he said, looking around the lobby, pulling at his shirt so it wouldn't cling to his back. Next to the registration desk was a huge espresso machine with dusty pipes that looked as if it hadn't worked for years. He couldn't believe this was the same hotel his mother had talked about constantly since his father died, the same hotel where his mother and father honeymooned in the twenties.

Liz walked over from the registration desk and took his mother's hand. "I got room twenty-two, Nonie, just like you wanted. Let's go up and get you dried off."

Nonie's white hair was wet and stiff over her eyes. She shivered. "Maybe this wasn't such a good idea, Elizabeth."

"We're going to have us a fine time," Liz said, then helped his mother up the stairs.

Verlin shook off the rain and rubbed his arms. "Hey, Liz, you mind telling me what our room number is?"

"*Ours* is twenty-two," she said. "*Yours* is twenty-five. Down the hall. Good night, Verlin."

In his room, Verlin threw his suitcase on the bed and watched it bounce to the floor. Instead of picking it up again, he sat on the bed, took off his wet shoes, and threw them smack against the wall.

He'd thought that nothing Liz could do would surprise him anymore. In May, his father died in Dallas when an aneurysm burst behind his left ear, and Liz invited his mother to move in with them. In June, their daughter Patty left her third drunk husband, and Liz invited her and the babies to move in, too. Then, in July, Liz told him that his vacation would be a trip down memory lane for Nonie. Now it was August. They were stuck in the ruins of a hotel, high in the mountains of Mexico, and Liz was sleeping with his mother. He didn't think he could take any more surprises.

He picked up the other suitcases and knocked on the door down the hall. Liz took them from him, then started to close the door.

He wedged his foot in the gap. "I'd like to talk to Mama."

The room was cold and damp. French doors opened onto the balcony. Outside a dozen green parakeets perched on the cast-iron rails, huddled together with their backs to the wall of rainwater that spilled from the awning overhead.

"Why are these doors open?" he said.

"Nonie's hot."

His mother sat on a wide bed with tall brass bedposts. She didn't look well. Her shoulders were hunched forward, and she seemed to have shrunk.

He closed the balcony doors. "Mama, I'm afraid Liz and I made a bad mistake bringing you here. If you want, we can leave tomorrow."

"We're not going anywhere, Verlin," his mother said. "This place may not seem like much to you, but Elizabeth and I've decided to stay."

Verlin stayed in bed with a cold the next day, while Liz and Nonie went to the market. At the hotel restaurant that night his mother looked better. She wore a homespun *mantla* cloth dress. She sipped Cardinal Mendoza brandy, joked and laughed, and ate duck in banana leaves, as she had on her honeymoon night. Verlin was surprised how good the food was, and he began to enjoy himself when his mother talked about the trip she and his father had taken fifty years before.

"I didn't want to leave this hotel," his mother said. "But Daddy wanted to drive down the mountain in a roadster. The roads were mud and we got stuck and then we argued for hours, but finally we made it to Papantla on the gulf coast. The Indians harvested vanilla beans from orchids, and the whole town smelled like vanilla. The beaches were white."

Nonie smiled.

"I think I'll call Patty," Liz said. "Check up on the babies."

"You mean, check up on Patty," Verlin said. He couldn't believe she'd brought Patty up.

"No, I didn't mean that. I meant just what I said."

"Like hell. You and I both know she's probably having a big bash at the house. Probably already gotten some drunk to propose to her again. I swear, that girl's life ambition is to have seven kids by seven different drunks."

Liz was standing. Nonie wasn't smiling anymore. She looked up from her plate and stared blankly at two Indian boys sitting at the next table, spreading catsup over their potato chips and eating them with their fingers. She turned to Verlin, tried to say something, then threw up.

In the cold room upstairs, Liz closed the balcony doors and covered Nonie with a blanket. Verlin wiped his pants with a wet towel.

"My God, Liz, of all the times to bring up Patty."

"You leave Liz alone," Nonie said, shivering and holding the blanket under her chin. "Make yourself useful and go to bed."

"That's a good idea, Verlin," Liz said.

"Look, Mama, I think we'd better call a doctor."

"Get away from me. I don't need a doctor."

"She's all right, Verlin. I'll stay up with her and she'll feel a lot better in the morning."

"Look, Liz, I'm telling you, I think we should call a—"

"Shut up, Verlin," his mother said.

Verlin marched to the door. "Christ, I'm going to bed."

Next morning at dawn, Liz came to his room and shook him awake.

"Verlin," she said, "I fell asleep."

He sat up in bed when he realized she was crying.

"Nonie's dead."

In the room down the hall, he paced around the brass bed where his mother lay. He stopped to cover her but changed his mind. He wanted to close her mouth and eyes, but he couldn't decide which to do first. Then Liz pulled the heavy blanket over his mother's face. The blanket had a simple Aztec design, a gray-brown bird with straight, hard wings.

"God," he said, "I can't believe this." He wanted to scream accusations at Liz. Instead, he slapped the brass ball on the bedpost hard with his open hand. His stinging palm calmed him some.

"We should call a doctor," Liz said. "And a priest. There are priests in that monastery we passed coming in."

"You want to call a doctor now? A doctor won't do Mama any good *now*. A priest sure as hell won't." He realized he was shouting.

"You have every right to be mad at me," Liz said, "but Nonie would want last rites. And we need to call the police. A funeral home. We've got arrangements to make."

"You've made all the arrangements you're going to make this trip, Liz. And for now, we don't call the police. We don't call anybody. Not until I've called the American consulate."

In the lobby, Verlin couldn't find a phone, and he wanted a cup of coffee more than anything he'd ever wanted in his life. When he asked the hotel clerk for a cup, the clerk just looked at the broken espresso machine and shrugged. "A phone, then," Verlin said and put his fist to his cheek. After he'd stood in the hotel phone booth for thirty minutes, the call from Mexico City finally came through.

"American consulate. Murray Smith here."

Verlin tried to explain.

"I'm sorry, Mr. Keeling, but from a U.S. consulate point of view there's no procedure for this kind of thing. We have many regulations on transporting the deceased from the U.S. to Mexico but nothing on transporting the deceased from Mexico to the U.S."

"You mean you can't help me."

"This isn't our jurisdiction. Since you're on Mexican soil, you'll have to follow Mexican procedures. Do you have plenty of money?"

"Five, six hundred dollars in traveler's checks. And some cash."

"That should be enough."

"For what?"

"*Mordida*, Mr. Keeling."

The hotel clerk knocked at the phone booth door and handed Verlin a yellowed packet of Sanka. Verlin looked at the clerk and asked Smith, "Mordida. What's this *mordida*?" The clerk waited with his palm open, and Verlin covered the phone. "Hot water, and a cup."

"It's the custom here in Mexico," Smith said. "You'll need to give certain people incentives to expedite getting something like this done."

"Bribes," Verlin said. "You mean bribes."

"If you give the right people the right incentives, Mr. Keeling, your mother will be out of the country in, say, three or four days. This is not a promise but a possibility. I'd suggest you take notes."

Verlin fumbled for the pad and pen in his pocket and began writing.

Smith explained that Verlin should first contact the local police, who would contact the medical examiner in Teziutlán and then take his mother's body to a local hospital. Since she'd died without medical attention, she'd have to have an autopsy.

"At the hospital, you'll need a death certificate and a hospital release form," Smith said. "Now, it's important that you make sure the medical examiner is a doctor. Then make sure he does the autopsy. A doctor has to do the autopsy, and the medical examiner has to sign the DC and release form and then write an embalming letter. You want to keep things simple."

Verlin was confused, but he wrote quickly.

Smith then explained that once the autopsy was finished the medical examiner would need something, ten or twenty dollars, to sign the death certificate. Then Verlin could have his mother's body sent to an embalmer. "Now, I have to caution you," Smith said. "Embalming techniques are not the best here in Mexico. Most embalmers use aspiration."

"Aspiration," Verlin said. He wrote that down.

"They stick a tube in the abdomen and suck out all the bodily fluids. Then they use a cavity chemical. You don't want that. There's no telling how long the deceased's body might be here in Mexico, and cavity chemicals don't preserve the extremities."

"Extremities," Verlin said and wrote down *extremities*.

Smith then explained the proper embalming procedures and how to get an embalming certificate from the local health department.

"Stop," Verlin said. His notes were all jumbled together.

"There's more," Smith said without a pause. Verlin could then have his mother's body sent to a funeral home. He should pay the undertaker for the casket and casket flight container, then should give the undertaker something to have the body flown air freight to El Paso or Brownsville. He would also have to give at least five percent of the undertaker's sale to the local deputies. Then the worst would be over. Verlin would be free to work out the details with American border officials.

"Have you got all that?" Smith said.

Verlin let the phone dangle from its cord when the clerk knocked at the door. He took the cup of hot water from the clerk and gave him a dollar, then waved him on and slammed the door. His hands were shaking. He crushed the hard Sanka packet in his fist, opened it into the cup, and stirred it with his pen. When he drank, the coffee tasted like burnt cork and scalded his mouth, and he spewed it all over himself and his notepad. He slammed the cup into the pay phone, where it shattered.

"You listen to me, goddammit," he shouted into the phone. "All I want to do is get my mother out of this country and get her a decent funeral."

At first, Verlin thought Smith had hung up. Then Smith said, "There *is* one other thing you could do, Mr. Keeling, but you didn't hear me say this. Do you have a car?"

"Sure, a lease car. An LTD, I think. A new seventy-two model."

"Good. That's fine. If I were you, Mr. Keeling, I'd put my mother in the trunk of that car and drive like hell out of Mexico. I wouldn't stop for anything."

The balcony doors were open again and the room was cold. Liz paced under the red tile awning and looked out at the rain. "What took you so long, Verlin? Did you call a doctor?"

He handed her the notepad.

"What's this?"

He told her.

"We can't take Nonie ourselves," Liz said. "Not like she is. What about the arrangements?"

"I already told you. We can't even *think* about arrangements until we get Mama across the border."

"We at least need to have her body prepared somehow."

"Look, Liz, I've been through all that, and that's why we don't have time to argue. There's a hard two-day drive to Matamoros, and I'm leaving when it gets dark. If you want to go with me, then pack your things and Mama's. If you don't, then let me know now. Patty can come get you."

Liz was quiet.

"Well, are you going with me?"

"Of course I'm going, but I think this is all a terrible mistake."

"This trip was *your* idea, Liz. Don't talk to me about mistakes."

The hotel clerk stopped sweeping the floor when he saw the twenty. Verlin pointed upstairs, then looked outside to see if Liz had pulled the car around to the porte cochere. When he saw the rental car's headlights, he motioned to the clerk, who followed him upstairs. His mother was wrapped in the thick gray blanket on the bed. Verlin pointed to the twenty, then to his mother's body, then downstairs. He put his finger to his lips. The clerk nodded.

Verlin hefted her stiff upper body, and the clerk lifted her feet. Verlin was surprised how heavy she was. He struggled to hold her, backed through the door and down the stairs. Soon they were outside.

"What are you waiting for, Liz? Open the trunk."

"No, Verlin."

He almost dropped his mother. "What?"

"I said no. You're not putting her back there."

"Where do you suggest we *put* her?" he said through his teeth.

"The backseat."

Verlin looked around to make sure no one was watching. "Liz, could we maybe not argue about this right now? Open the goddamn trunk."

"I'll cover her up, Verlin."

They laid his mother in the backseat, and Liz covered her with the two Indian ponchos and blankets from Verlin's bed. Verlin put the suitcases on top of the pile, to cover his mother better, then handed the clerk the twenty.

"Get in," he told Liz.

Starting the car, he turned it onto Avenida Hidalgo and toward the outskirts of Teziutlán. A fine rain had sheeted the narrow cobbled lanes, making them black and glossy in the town's lights.

He was too angry to say anything for the hour it took to drive the mountain road winding down to the gulf. At Nautla, he turned north onto the narrow highway running along an open stretch of white beach, where the sea wind whipped coco palms along the shore. He turned on the overhead light and checked the map.

"Where are we?" Liz said.

"Not far from Tecolutla. We've got to cross a river by ferry to get there. I just hope it's still running this late." He looked at his watch. "Christ, eleven o'clock."

The rain stopped and the full moon broke through the scudding clouds. The city's lights reflected off the river a few miles ahead.

"Look, Liz, I've been thinking," he said. "I was going to tell you this when we got home, but I don't see much point in putting it off now. Don't get me wrong. For now, we need to get Mama home. We need to stick with each other till then. But after Mama's buried next to Daddy at Restland, I'm leaving you."

"Oh, is that a fact? I thought I was leaving you."

"You were? Who says?"

"Patty's made the suggestion a few times the last couple of months. Even *Nonie* has. And the thought's crossed my mind." Liz leaned toward him in her seat. "Look, Verlin, why are you blaming me for all this? Do you think I *planned* what's happened?"

"This doesn't have anything to do with what's happened."

"You really expect me to believe that? All right, okay, so you're leaving me. That's settled. Now, I want to know why." She sat back in her seat and folded her arms.

He leaned against the steering wheel. "Mainly, Liz, I'm just tired."

"Oh, that's priceless," she said. "I can hear it now. 'Hello, Patty? It's Mom. Just called to tell you we're on our way home. Oh, and by the way, honey, you might also want to know: Nonie's dead and your father's leaving me. What's that? Why? Why, your father's tired, honey. That's all. No need to worry.'"

"I told you at the hotel, Liz. If you're staying with me, you're not calling Patty."

"I'm calling her the next town I see a phone."

"Fine, call her. But you do and she'll have to come get you."

"You wouldn't leave me. Not out here."

"You call Patty and you're on your own. It's that simple."

They were still shouting at each other when the road came to a dead end at the Río Tecolutla. He pumped the brakes, but the car went into a skid on the crushed shell surface and stopped just short of the ferry dock. A soldier with a rifle slung over his shoulder stood at the dock's end in the car's headlights. Verlin looked at Liz, then watched the approaching soldier, who made a cranking motion with his hand.

Verlin rolled his window down. "We were just talking."

The soldier looked into the backseat. Verlin tried to smile.

"Legumbres," the soldier said.

Verlin made a face at Liz, but she shrugged. "The glove box, Liz. The book. Look up *legumbres*, for God's sake."

Liz fumbled in the glove box, found *Terry's Guide to Mexico*, and flipped through the pages while Verlin tried to explain that he and Liz were tourists. The soldier laughed. Then Verlin tried to think of a way to keep the soldier from searching the car. "The ferry. Does the ferry run again tonight?"

The soldier nodded, then pointed out to the river, at the red lights of the ferry coming toward them. Then the soldier looked behind the car. Verlin imagined hundreds of soldiers surrounding the car, but he looked into the rearview mirror and saw nothing.

Liz started laughing. "Vegetables. He wants to know if we have any vegetables."

Verlin said, "Shut up, Liz," but she continued to laugh wildly. He handed the soldier a ten and said, "No legumbres."

They were across the river in thirty minutes, and on the other side of Tecolutla he saw an old phone booth. He pulled off the beach road and stopped the car. He opened Liz's door, took out her luggage, and waited. Liz remained seated but didn't look at him. The surf roared behind him.

"Believe it or not," Liz shouted, "I can still remember a time when you weren't a complete bastard."

"That must have been before you turned our home into a halfway house."

"So you're going to blame me for that, too. What did you expect me to do, turn Nonie and Patty away?"

"Don't give me that Good Samaritan crap. You told Mama to sell her house. And Patty's twenty-eight years old. You had other reasons."

Liz crossed her legs in the front seat and stared at the dashboard. "Sure," she said, "I wanted someone to talk to."

"What's that supposed to mean?"

"Talking. Not *yelling* or *not talking* at all. You know, talking. There was a time when we talked."

"You want someone to talk to?" he said. "Tell you what, I'll call Patty for you. I'll be awful and she can come get you. Then you two can have a fine time on the way home, *talking* about what a bastard I was for abandoning you. And I can have a little peace for a change."

She didn't make any move to get out of the car, so he picked up the suitcases to return them to the backseat.

"Leave them," she said. She got out of the car and walked to the phone booth, then reached into her purse. He carried the suitcases over to the booth and watched her rummage through her wallet.

"You have any change?" she said.

He gave her several pesos, then counted out three hundred dollars in traveler's checks and handed them to her. For a moment, she didn't seem to know what to do with them. Then she stuffed them inside her purse and walked into the phone booth. When she started dialing, he started the engine.

After driving for fifteen minutes, watching the tall clumps of pampas grass along the highway pass into the sweep of the headlights, he stopped the car in the middle of the highway. He struck the dashboard with his fist.

"Christ, I can't." He turned the car around.

Her suitcases were still by the booth when he got there, but Liz was gone. Then he saw her walking along the beach. He put her luggage back into the car and sat on the car hood until she walked back.

"Patty wasn't home," she said, then sat in the car. He waited until she'd stopped crying before he got back into the car again.

Later, sometime after three in the morning, they passed through Papantla, and he smelled the faint scent of vanilla. He looked into the backseat, then at Liz, glad that she'd fallen asleep.

Even before the sun came up, the day was hot and humid in the marshy gulf lowlands. The smell of the sea gave way to another of sulfur and oil, and hundreds of oil wells and gas flare-offs lit up the hazy dark. Liz was snoring, strands of red hair wet with sweat and falling over her eyes. Verlin shifted constantly in the driver's seat to stay awake. He wanted a cup of coffee. Just after dawn outside Poza Rica, Liz woke up and rolled down her window. Her shirt was dark with sweat.

"I need to go to the bathroom," she said.

"We'll stop in Poza Rica. We're low on gas, and I've got to get this air conditioner fixed. The damn thing's not working. Maybe we should get some bags of ice. I don't know what'll happen if Mama gets ripe on us in this heat."

"My God, Verlin."

"All right, I'm sorry. I'm sorry for everything." He waited for her to respond but she didn't. "What do you want, Liz? I said I was sorry."

"Let's not talk about it anymore. Let's just take Nonie home."

At a Pemex station in Poza Rica, a mechanic slammed the car hood and said he could get a rebuilt compressor in two days. When Verlin told him he didn't have that long, the mechanic suggested a station on the border.

"Matamoros?" Verlin said. The attendant nodded. "That's no good."

The sun was already hot above the brown refinery haze. While Liz went to the restroom, Verlin leaned against the back door to make sure the attendant filling the car didn't get too close. He watched a goat chew on an oily dipstick rag next to the gas pump.

Parked at an angle on the shoulder across the station was a Day-Glo yellow Volkswagen bus. A headband hung from the rearview mirror, and a sticker on the white bumper said, *America, Love It or Leave It.* Verlin almost felt like talking to the owners of the van. They were hippies, but at least they were Americans. Then he saw two haggard Mexicans lean out of the open door at the side of the bus. One of them walked to the edge of the highway, looked at the rental car, watched a car pass, then looked at the rental car again.

Liz came around from the side of the station.

"Lock it up and roll up the windows," Verlin said.

"What for? It's already a hundred degrees in that car."

"Now."

While he paid the attendant inside the station, Verlin watched the Mexican cross the street and walk around the car. The man smiled at Liz through her window, then leaned down to look into the backseat. Liz reached across the seat to unlock Verlin's door. He started the car and pulled out of the station fast, the tires kicking up sand around the man in the rearview mirror.

"What was *that* all about?" A line of sweat made a *V* on Liz's blouse.

"I don't know. You see any hippies in a ditch somewhere, just don't tell me, all right?"

"What are you talking about? He was only smiling at me."

"You're unbelievable," he said. Then he was aware of the odor. He looked at Liz. "Do you smell that?"

"It's just all the refineries, Verlin." She shook her head. "It can't be Nonie. She's only been dead for—"

"Two days, Liz. Mama's been dead for two days."

They both looked at each other, then rolled their windows down. Hot air swirled into the car. Verlin looked into the mirror again.

"That van's behind us," he said. "I think they're following us."

Liz looked through the back window. "Why? Why would they do that?"

"Maybe they want our money." He glanced at her. "Maybe they want you."

It was late afternoon before they reached the outskirts of Tampico, and the Volkswagen van was still behind them. Liz had fallen back to a restless sleep again, and he caught himself nodding off two or three times. The hot blast of air coming through the window kept him awake, but he knew the odor was real now. It had settled into his lungs. When it finally became too much for him, he woke Liz.

"We've got to do something about that smell. Maybe there's something in the suitcases."

Liz knelt in the front seat and faced the back. She opened their suitcases and got out his Right Guard and her Chanel No. 5. While she sprayed the back of the car, he caught himself looking at the sweaty tightness of her khaki pants. It was almost dark when Liz sat back in her seat, and Verlin saw the van only a few car lengths behind them, its headlights on high beam.

"What's that idiot doing?" Verlin said.

Liz looked back. "Maybe he's trying to pass us."

Verlin slowed down to let the van pass but it didn't. It moved closer, a car length behind them. He pumped the brakes to make the van back off, but instead it moved in closer.

Tampico's lights were in the distance, and just ahead a tall neon sign blinked *Camino Real, Camino Real*. Verlin said, "Hold on, Liz," then swerved sharply left into the asphalt parking lot. The car skidded to a stop, and he watched the van pass out of sight.

The Camino Real Motor Inn looked American. The office and restaurant had an orange metal roof like a Howard Johnson's and a wide courtyard encircling a pool.

"We're stopping here," Verlin said. "We can only stay a couple of hours, but we can at least get cleaned up and get some sleep. Let that van get a few hundred miles the hell away from here. We'll leave later tonight when it's cooler. We'll have to leave Mama in the car." He waited for Liz to object, but her eyes were big and she looked shaken.

The motel room's air conditioner was on high, and he stood next to it in his underwear. Liz had gone to wash her hands but had been in the bathroom for thirty minutes. He opened the bathroom door and said, "Hurry it up, will you?"

He saw her naked silhouette in the shower and went in to wipe the mirror with a towel. After he washed his hands, he decided to shave before the mirror fogged again. He watched Liz turn under the water in the shower while he shaved. Then he walked to the shower door.

"Mind if I join you?" he said.

"Yes."

"Yes you mind, or yes I can?"

She opened the door a crack and said, "Get out of here, Verlin."

Twenty minutes later she came out. "You can go in now."

When he'd showered, Liz was sitting up in the bed, reading *Terry's Guide to Mexico* in her lap. He sat at the edge of the bed and kissed her wet hair. She closed the book. "No, Verlin." She sat in a chair next to the bed. "Nonie's dead, and you're leaving me, remember?"

"I remember."

"You go ahead and sleep. I'll stay up and wake you up when it's time to go."

"You don't have to do that, Liz. We can get a wake-up call. And I'll lay off. You need to get some sleep, too."

"It's just a couple of hours," she said. "I'm not sleepy."

Liz shook him awake.

"Verlin, I fell asleep."

He sat up in the bed. The air-conditioning was still running on high and the room was cold, but bright sunlight came in through the curtains.

"Christ, what time is it?" He reached for his watch on the nightstand. "It's past noon, Liz."

He jumped from the bed and rushed to get dressed. Liz stuffed clothes into their suitcases.

"I can't believe this," he said. "Do you realize how hot that car is by now? We'll *have* to put Mama in the trunk."

Liz threw one of her blouses into a suitcase and started to cry.

"Stop it, Liz." He walked to her and gripped her arms. "It's not your fault. None of this is your fault. Just finish packing and I'll check on Mama."

He opened the motel door and saw that the parking space in front of the room was empty. "Liz, did you move the car last night?"

"No, why would I do that?"

He ran out into the parking lot. Two cars were parked in front of the motel office, but the rest of the lot was empty. He ran around the swimming pool and saw the Volkswagen bus parked behind the pump house. He opened one of the van's side doors. Except for a discarded mescal bottle and a couple of dirty beach towels, the van was empty. He wiped the dust from the driver's window and looked inside. The headband still hung from the rearview mirror. The keys were in the ignition. He got into the van, started it, and drove around to the room.

Liz was standing outside the door. She let out a scream when she saw Verlin driving the van.

"The car's gone," he said. "Those bastards, they wanted the car. You still have those traveler's checks in your purse?"

"Yes, but what about Nonie?"

"Go pay for the room while I get our bags. Now."

When they drove out of the motel parking lot and onto the beach highway, he said, "We don't have much time. They were probably in a big hurry when they left, but it won't take them long to find out about Mama."

"Maybe they'll get rid of the car when they do."

"Or get rid of Mama. That's what I'm afraid of. Christ, Liz, she could be just about anywhere."

Then he saw the long black skid marks swerving from the highway to the shoulder, then down into the culvert. He pulled over to the side of the highway. The van's engine rattled at idle.

"What are you doing, Verlin?"

"There," he said. "Down there."

A cloud of flies hovered in the ditch. Verlin covered his mouth with his handkerchief and moved in closer. He lifted the beach towel slung over the bloated shape, then tossed the towel into the black ditch water. He started to gag. In the hot sun, the gray blanket had stretched taut. He backed up to the road and turned to Liz.

"I don't think anyone's seen her yet," he said. "We've got to hurry."

"I'll come down and help you."

"No, Liz. Pull the van in closer and warn me if any cars pass."

"You can't do it by yourself."

"Goddammit, don't argue with me."

He took a few deep breaths and held the last one. Then he walked to the body, waved the flies away, and worked his hands under the stiff blanket until he'd gotten a good grip. He strained under the weight. As he lay his mother's body inside the van, he felt a sharp pain in the small of his back and let out his breath as if he'd been kicked there. He crawled over his mother into the back of the van, dragged her there, and stumbled into the driver's seat, gasping for air at the window.

Liz slammed the side doors and got in on the passenger side, and he drove the van onto the highway north. On the other side of Tampico he stopped in front of a dry goods store and told Liz to get out of the van while he went inside. He came out with a shovel and a coil of rope. Twenty minutes later he turned the van onto an old caliche road that cut west into the mountains running parallel with the beach. He drove another thirty minutes on rough mountain roads.

Liz said, "Over there, Verlin, by those trees."

"It's a long walk, Liz."

"It's a good place."

He dragged his mother's body to the edge of the van bed, and Liz helped him lower her to the ground. He couldn't straighten up. He laid his hand at the small of his back.

"What's the matter, Verlin?"

"I think I pulled something."

She reached for his arm, but he pulled away. "Don't, for chrissake. I'm all right."

He uncoiled the rope and cut it into two equal lengths, then moved back to tie one length around his mother's shoulders and the other around her feet. Out of range of the odor, he pulled the rope tight around the blanket and said, "You'll have to help me with this, Liz." He handed her one length of rope and they both pulled.

It was late afternoon when they reached the stand of pines. There were fewer rocks now, and the flat layer of pine needles on sand made the pulling easier. He walked to the van to get the shovel, then returned.

"Where?" he asked Liz.

She walked to a spot under an outcropping of rock clear of pine roots. "Here."

He dug into the hard-packed sand. About two feet down, he struck a big rock, dug around it, and pried it free with the shovel. Then Liz helped him pull it from the hole. He dug again for a while but stopped and lay back on the flat ground, his feet dangling into the hole.

"It's your back," Liz said.

"I'm just resting, Liz."

"Let me have the shovel."

When she stepped into the hole, he let her take the shovel and watched her dig for half an hour. Then he took over. They took turns until the hole was above Liz's waist.

The sun was almost down. He took the shovel from Liz and laid it aside. He grasped her wrist and opened her hand. An open blister caked with sand and clay ran along the inside of her palm.

"That's deep enough," he said.

They dragged his mother to the edge of the hole, then pulled a fallen pine to the other side. After he stretched the rope over the trunk and Liz pulled the ends tight, he nudged his mother's body over the edge and took one of the ropes from Liz. Then they eased her down until the ropes became slack and she lay at the bottom.

Liz took a handful of sand and held it in her palm. He took another, started to drop it into the hole, then stopped.

"You go ahead, Liz."

When they'd finished, he said, "We'd better hurry now." He looked down into the hole, then dropped in a shovelful of sand, which covered the Aztec bird on the blanket. Liz scooped sand with both hands and tossed it in. By the time they'd finished filling the hole and spreading pine needles over the fresh dirt, the moon was well up over the dark mountains.

"We should mark the place," Liz said, and together they rolled the big rock to the head of his mother's grave.

Later, back on the coastal highway north, Liz said, "Verlin, how do we explain all this?"

"We don't," he said. "We can't. We just have to lie."

"You want me to drive?"

"Not just yet," he said. "In a while."

Just after dawn, they reached Matamoros. Liz parked the van in a barrio side street two blocks from the Río Grande bridge checkpoint. She came around and opened the van's side doors, then took out their suitcases.

"Leave them," Verlin said.

He pulled the airline identification tags from the luggage handles and ripped the tags up, then tossed the suitcases into the brown water of a nearby drainage ditch.

Liz folded her arms. "You could've at least let me *change* first." Her shoes and the knees of her gabardine slacks were still caked with the sand and clay. There were salt circles under her arms.

He shrugged.

On the main street, Liz stopped in front of a curio shop window just before they reached the bridge. She pointed up to a top shelf on the other side of the glass. He followed her inside the shop, reached to the shelf, and pulled down a heavy gray urn covered with dust. The shopkeeper seemed surprised when Verlin paid the full twenty dollars without haggling.

They walked along the sidewalk of the bridge crossing the Río Grande and passed by the long line of cars waiting at the customs checkpoint. A border guard at the sidewalk gate said, "You folks got any alcoholic beverages or vegetables?"

"No vegetables," Verlin said. He opened the urn and tilted it so that the guard could see inside. "We're parked on the Texas side."

"Car's safer over there," the guard said.

Verlin nodded and paid the duty tax.

Then they crossed over into Brownsville.

Verlin spotted a cab and hailed it. "The airport," he said.

At the airport terminal, they stopped at the Hertz Rent A Car desk. Verlin broke through the line and shouted at the woman behind the counter, "Somebody stole my goddamn car in Matamoros last night. Threw us in a ditch, took our luggage, everything."

The woman reached under the counter for a form. "Why didn't you call us from there?"

Verlin leaned over the desk. "Are you crazy? My wife and I were lucky to get out of there alive. Just look at us. I want another car. Now."

"You'll have to go to the end of the line, sir."

"Go to the end of the line, hell. This is the last time I rent one of your goddamn cars."

The woman jotted down something on the form. "What's your name, sir?"

As they walked away from the desk, Verlin gave the keys to Liz. "You think I overdid it?"

"Just a little."

They passed a row of pay phones outside the airport restaurant, and he took Liz's arm. "Why don't we get some breakfast?" he said. "And some coffee. I could really use a cup of coffee."

"You go on in. I need to call Patty."

He let go of her arm.

"By now she's probably worried, Verlin. And I have to let her know something."

"Just what are you going to *tell* her?"

"That she needs to start looking for a new place to live. That Nonie's dead and we're taking her home."

"I'll be waiting for you in the restaurant."

———————

Just after Liz drove the rental car across the bridge from the mainland to South Padre Island, Verlin fell asleep in the passenger seat. She woke him an hour later. "I think this is a good place."

They both got out of the car and walked over tall white dunes to an empty beach. Liz laid the urn in the sand, and they walked together along the edge of the surf, combing the beach for driftwood. When they'd gathered enough wood, he made a fire, and they sat facing the sea, their backs to the flames.

After the fire had lost its heat and they'd filled the urn with ash, Verlin faced his wife. "Liz, did Mama really tell you to leave me?"

"It doesn't matter now, Verlin."

"You know, the last thing she said to me was 'Shut up.'"

Liz knelt in the sand. "Shut up, Verlin."

He stood and walked into the waves, then bent to wash the clay from his knees and the ash from his hands. When he came back, he said, "Liz, we need to talk."

She picked up the urn. "I'm ready," she said.

Fair Day

For John

Chase and Larry Garrett's father left home a year ago. This time last October, he took three suits on wooden hangers and a stack of shoe boxes, and he hasn't been back since. Chase talked to his father just once, over the phone. That was sometime in July. His father said something about visitation and coming by the house to pick up Chase and Larry for a weekend together at Corpus Christi. But the man never showed up.

Three months later, when he finally does come by the house, Chase's father doesn't come inside. Chase and Larry are both sitting cross-legged on the den floor watching "The Fugitive" when, through the picture window, Chase sees his father duck out of the passenger side of a blue Karmann Ghia and walk up the driveway to the house. Chase runs to the foyer to open the front door. Larry follows behind.

Their father stands on the porch under the yellow bug light, his balding forehead bruised and covered with tiny scratches, a wide Band-Aid crimped over the bridge of his nose, one of his eyes black and swollen shut. "Is your mother home?" he says, smiling, like a vacuum salesman.

"She's washing dishes," Chase says. "Hey, what happened? You get in a fight or something?"

"Yeah," Larry says.

"No, I didn't get in a fight."

"So, hey," Chase says, "you taking us somewhere, or what?"

"No, I just need to talk to your mother. Go get your mother, will you?"

Their mother shows up at the door, drying her hands with a dish towel. She tells Chase and Larry to go to their bedrooms, but instead they go back to the den and turn the TV down. On the screen the one-armed man squints in the shadows while their mother and father shout at each other.

"You're three months late on your child support," she starts off.

"I'm taking the station wagon," he says.

"What? Why? What's wrong with your car?"

"I totaled it on Central Expressway."

"Why can't you take *her* car?"

Their father glances back at the Karmann Ghia parked at the curb, then back to their mother. "Her insurance doesn't cover me. Look, Ann, she doesn't have anything to do with this. Leave her out of this, will you?"

"You can't take my car, Gil," their mother says. "How in God's name am I supposed to get to work?"

"I've got to work, too, you know."

"What, so you can pay your child support, right?"

"Look, I pay the house payments every month. I pay the payments on that station wagon. I just wanted to tell you I was taking it. I didn't have to tell you, you know. I still have my keys."

"I'm calling my lawyer," their mother says.

"So call him." Their father turns around and walks down the porch steps, cutting across the grass to the driveway.

"But, God, Gil, how am I supposed to get to work?" Their mother holds her head with her hands, the way she does sometimes.

"The bus," he tells her. "Take the bus."

That's it, the last thing Chase hears his father say. The man doesn't come inside and talk to Chase the way he's imagined it would happen. His father opens the station wagon door and gets inside, slams the door shut, and backs the car down the driveway. The woman sitting in the blue Karmann Ghia makes a U at the curb and follows the station wagon down the street.

Chase watches both sets of taillights pass behind the Nelsons' willow at the corner of the block.

"Man, what a load of crap," he says. "Jesus."

"Yeah," Larry says next to him.

Chase turns off "The Fugitive" and waits for the crying to start, but it never does. His mother just goes to bed. Next morning, she stays there. She doesn't get up to go to work. She doesn't get him and Larry up to fix them breakfast or to take them to school. Over the next few days, she gets up a few times to eat a bowl of tomato soup or to go to the bathroom, but a week later, when Fair Day comes at school, she's still in bed.

That morning, Chase gets himself up and shakes Larry awake, like he's been doing all week. He showers, dresses, and slaps his face with some Aramis his father left behind in the medicine cabinet. In the kitchen he reaches down a bowl and a spoon, then the Fruit Loops and the carton of milk he bought the day before at the 7–11 down at the Casa Linda Shopping Center. He goes back to Larry's room and shakes Larry awake again.

"Come on, man, get up, will you? We'll be late for the bus. We'll have to walk to school again."

"Don't want to get up," Larry says. His left eye is glued shut. His eyelids peel open slowly from the corner of his eye.

"It's Fair Day, man. You don't want to miss Fair Day, do you?"

"Yeah."

"Look, I'm counting to three, and if you don't get up, I'm ripping your stupid face off." Chase fists his knuckles up under Larry's chin. "One. Two."

"Go 'head, hit me," Larry says.

"All right. Okay. Jesus." Chase rocks back on his heels and holds his head with his hands, then holds his hands down to his sides so he won't use them. He paces around the room, stepping over Larry's dirty sweatshirts and underwear and Tonka trucks. "Tell you what, man. This is the deal. You get up and I'll take you to the freak show. How's that? They got all kinds of weird stuff in there."

"Like what?"

"Dead babies floating around in bottles, deformed people with their ears where their noses are supposed to go, shit like that."

"Yeah," Larry says, then throws the sheets back.

Chase digs through the piles of overturned Hot Wheels and wadded Levis and half-naked G.I. Joes on the floor till he finds Larry's favorite pair of bell-bottoms, the ones he's been wearing all week. They're still stiff with dried mud and they're too big for Larry, but Chase doesn't want to argue with him again all morning over a pair of stupid bell-bottoms. Chase holds them out while Larry steps into them and yawns and holds his arms up for the last clean sweatshirt in his dresser drawer. Then Larry sits on the bed swinging his legs, and Chase tells him to hold his legs still, so he can tie his stupid shoes. When he's finished, Chase looks up to see that Larry's fallen back onto the bed, asleep again.

While Larry's eating his bowl of Fruit Loops in the kitchen, Chase starts throwing all the clothes scattered around Larry's room under the bed, until he uncovers the black bald spot next to the closet where Larry burned the shag rug with the kitchen matches a few days before. Then Chase remembers and pulls all the clothes out from under Larry's bed again, tossing them into a pile over the carpet's burnt spot, just in case their mother finally gets up today and wanders into Larry's room.

Chase stops at Larry's dresser to look at the laminated Mobil photo I.D. his father used to clip onto his shirt pocket mornings before he left for work. In the photo, his father is turning his head to look off at something, and his face is blurred like he's under water. Next to the I.D., leaning against Larry's Creature from the Black Lagoon model on the dresser, is a smudged Polaroid of Larry squinting at the camera in the bright sun and holding up a tiny perch he caught with his Zebco at Lake Texoma. The shadow of his father, holding up the camera to snap the shot, stretches out on the beach at Larry's bare feet.

In the kitchen, Chase puts Larry's bowl and spoon into the sink, with all the other bowls and spoons, and drops the empty Fruit Loops box into the A & P sack under the sink. Then he leads Larry to their mother's bedroom door, opens it a crack, and looks inside.

"Up yet?" Larry whispers behind him.

"Don't think so, man. Look, I'm going in. We got to get us some more cash. It's the last twenty bucks, so we can't spend it all, all right? We got to save some, for more Fruit Loops and shit."

"Yeah," Larry says.

Chase opens the purse on his mother's dresser and gets her wallet out while Larry waits outside. Chase finds four five-dollar bills inside and some change. He takes out two of the bills and then gets an extra one just in case, and then changes his mind again and puts the extra one back in her wallet. He's careful when he snaps the wallet shut, but it makes too much noise anyway, and his mother moves in the bed behind him.

"You getting up?" Chase says.

"Maybe," she says. "In a while."

"It's Fair Day at school," he says.

"Good."

"I didn't take much but we needed some. That okay?"

"Fine," she says.

"See you later." He starts to leave, but then she sits up in the bed. She's got pink creases on her face from the pillow, like a map of Africa. "Chase, you and Larry be careful, all right? You watch him close. And watch your language."

"Sure thing, Mom. No sweat."

Later that morning, when they're riding in the school bus downtown, Chase tells Larry how they'll meet up at the fair. Larry's with the first-grade group and he's with the sixth-grade group, and he tells Larry that when all the classes meet up at Big Tex around noon, the two of them will sneak off together.

"That way," he tells Larry, "I can keep an eye on you."

Chase pulls out one of the five-dollar bills wadded in his back pocket and hands it to Larry. "Now, look, man. Don't spend this unless you got to. The midway's got a lot of stupid games, and I don't want you spending this money on crap. The rides are free with our school tickets so just use this if you get hungry, okay?"

"Yeah," Larry says.

The bus drives through East Dallas, past an old black man sitting on a car seat in the dirt yard of his leaning gray house. At an intersection, the bus turns left past a concrete-block building with an unlit neon sign over a padded black door that says *All Nude Girls*. Then the bus passes under a sun-faded billboard with a balding man who smiles down at Chase and says, in a big cartoon bubble, *Smiling Joe's Insurance. He Covers All Losses, Large and Small.* The next block down, the bus turns under the *State Fair of Texas* arch and drives past the museums and the ponds, where the willows hang down over the water and the families all sit on green benches with crumpled lunch sacks in their laps.

The kids file out of the bus, and Chase watches from behind as Larry walks off with the first-grade group. Larry's jeans hang low on his hips so that Chase can see the striped elastic band of his skivvies and the crease between his cheeks. The seat of his drooping jeans is black with flaky clay, the bells on his jeans are all muddy around the edges where they drag the ground, and they're frayed behind where he keeps stepping on them with the heels of his loafers, pulling them down even farther.

"Jesus," Chase says. He decides to catch up with Larry to pull his pants up, but then he sees Larry hitch them up himself and hears Mr. Henley, the sixth-grade teacher, shout, "Let's all stick together, troops. Don't want any missing persons around here."

Chase falls in behind his class. Under his shoes the street is sticky with chewing gum and bubbles of hot asphalt and smears of catsup and mustard and spilled Coke. Everything smells like corn-dog grease and cotton candy and his father's old work shirts. Big Tex stands high up above the midway, holding his arm straight out and pointing at nothing, his giant cowboy hat and boots painted concrete, his huge red cowboy shirt billowing and flapping in the wind like sheets on a clothesline, the hinge of his jaw broken and hanging open. A shadow passes overhead like a cloud. Chase looks up at the cable cars with the people inside laughing down at him, and he wonders if he could spit from that high up.

Mr. Henley leads the sixth-grade class to the exposition center, where hundreds of shining cars rotate on stands with girls who can't stop smiling in their red miniskirts and their plastic go-go boots. They run their fingers along the cars' sharp fenders and try to make their voices sound throaty through microphones that feed back and echo down the long aisles to the stage. Mr. Henley stops the group at the display of a see-through engine. He points at the spinning radiator fan, at the pistons that move up and down, and tries to explain how everything works.

A country band finishes playing "Waltz across Texas" on the bandstand, and the bald emcee walks up to the mike. "Remember, folks, to sign up now for the grand prize. The drawing is at seven o'clock tonight and"—the emcee shouts—"*you must be present to win.*" Below the bandstand is a new sixty-eight Shelby Cobra GT convertible with wide stripes and an air scoop on the hood and a spoiler in the back, and next to that is a go-cart with a fiberglass Mustang body like the car's. Two tumblers are covered with chicken wire and filled with white sweepstakes forms, one next to the car, the other next to the go-cart. A fat junior high kid sits inside the go-cart with his knees rammed in up to his chest.

Mr. Henley turns around, and Chase leaves his group to give the go-cart a closer look. He finds a stubby pencil next to the entry box, picks up a few sweepstakes forms for the go-cart, and fills in his name and address. Then he writes out one for Larry and stands on his toes to drop it into the tumbler next to the go-cart. He feels a hand on his shoulder and turns around.

"Stay with the group, will you?" Mr. Henley says, then takes the sixth-grade class to the midway to ride the Texas Tornado and the Tilt-a-Whirl and the Martian Spider. When Chase's class comes back to Big Tex at noon, the first-grade group is there but Larry isn't. Larry's teacher doesn't seem to notice he's gone. Chase waits till Mr. Henley looks the other way and goes back to the midway to look for Larry.

———————————

At the freak tent, the hawker stands under the sagging canvas signs and barks at the crowd, "He crawled out of the bayou and they tried to civilize him. Come see the Alligator Man. Only one dollar." The opening into the tent is dark, the sawdust scattered on the ground inside is yellow and damp, and the place smells like a horse stall. Chase doesn't see Larry and decides not to go in.

After a while he stops looking and watches a kid turn a crank to move a little crane behind a glass box full of pocket radios and watches with plastic wristbands. The crane's three-fingered hand opens over an imitation survival knife, then jerks and drops and snaps closed around the pile next to the knife. When the kid cranks the crane up, a cast-metal car comes up with it, but then the car slips out of the crane's steel fingers and the kid shouts, "Dad!"

Just then, Chase sees Larry under the striped awning of a tent across the midway, throwing rings from behind a long table.

"Hey, man, where you been?" Chase says, winded from running through the crowd.

Larry doesn't look at him but throws a metal ring toward rows of Coke bottles spray-painted blue and red and green. The ring misses the bottles and falls to the concrete floor, spinning to a stop like a mayonnaise lid. Larry kicks the leg of the long table, and the tabletop shivers.

"How much you spend so far?" Chase says, hiking Larry's drooping bell-bottoms up from behind.

"Still got some."

"I told you not to spend money on this shit," Chase says.

Larry points at a monkey doll almost as big as he is that grins down from the shelf above the rows of bottles. "Trying to get that," he says.

"What for?"

"Mom."

"Here, let me give it a try." Chase buys three rings from a woman with a light gray mustache that curls out over the corners of her mouth. "Which one?" Chase asks her, and she points at the red bottle in the middle. "No sweat," Chase says.

Twenty minutes later, after he's already spent most of his five dollars, he's rung only one bottle, a green one in front. "One more try, man, and that's it." He buys his last three rings and hooks one of the blue bottles in the front row.

"Yeah," Larry says. "More."

"No, that's it, that's all." Chase turns to the lady with the mustache and asks her, "Okay, so what we get?" She hands him a palm-sized plastic monkey that smokes pin-sized cigarettes.

"What a crock," he says.

"Yeah," Larry says.

Chase slips the monkey into his back pocket. "All right, okay, let's go to the fun house or something. Jesus."

"Want to go to the freak tent," Larry says, kicking the table leg again.

"We can't go there now, man. We just blew too much money. Now, let's go. And stick with me, will you?"

They thread through the crowd. When Chase gets to the Bavarian Fun House, he looks back to check on Larry, but Larry's not behind him anymore. Chase hurries to the freak show and sees Larry run behind the tent and slip under one of the tent's closed flaps. Chase ducks under the rope and slides under the flap himself, then waits for his eyes to get used to the dark, for his nose to get used to the horse-stall smell.

He looks around inside for Larry. In the stall behind the first canvas partition, he sees a goat with gnarled and scabby wings, but the wings look like they've been glued on. Behind the next partition he finds Larry alone, looking up at the Alligator Man.

"I swear to God, man," Chase says, "I'm going to tear your stupid face off."

Larry doesn't look at him. "Doesn't look like a al-gator."

Chase looks at the Alligator Man in his dark stall. Half his face hangs over itself in bumpy folds like the deflated moldy grapefruit Chase found in the back of the refrigerator six months after his father left. The Alligator Man reaches a curled hand out of the shadows and scratches himself on the knee. Chase looks away and pulls Larry's pants up by the belt loops from behind. "Let's go. Stinks like shit in here."

"Yeah," Larry says.

At the Bavarian Fun House, Chase and Larry tumble inside the rolling beer barrels, then wait a long time for the air jets to blow up girls' dresses, but no girls in dresses show up. Then they dig around in their pockets and split a foot-long corn dog and a Dr. Pepper with the change they have left over. An hour later, it's their turn in line for the cable car. The attendant swings a car around and latches the door behind them. They have the car all to themselves.

The car jerks up at an angle, swinging back and forth on the steel cable. Larry holds on to the window bars and shouts, "Yeah," down at the people. Then the car levels off and the wind picks up, and they hang out and look down at the Cotton Bowl and Big Tex and the midway below.

Chase spits out over the side in a long arc, but his spit scatters in the wind.

"Shit," he says, "too far down."

Larry spits over the side, too, and says, "Yeah."

As the cable car passes over the freak tent below, Chase looks out at the skyline. He spots the Southland Life building downtown, then the winged red horse flying on the scaffolding over the roof of the Mobil building. He points it out to Larry.

"See that red horse over there? That's where *he* works."

Larry looks at him.

"He took us up there one time," Chase says. "Up to his office. It was up on the twenty-fifth floor, I remember. Then he took us up on the roof to see that big red horse. Remember that?"

Larry shakes his head.

"Didn't think so, man. You were just a kid."

Larry looks down at the cable car floor. He shuffles his feet and looks at his loafers a while. Then he kicks the cable car door, and the window bars rattle in their frames.

"Hate him," Larry says. "Hate his guts." He spits again, but this time the spit dribbles down his chin and onto his shirt. He looks down at the spit on his shirt and wipes at it and smears it all over the front of his shirt with the back of his hand.

"Oh, man," Chase says. "Here. Come here." He pulls his handkerchief out of his back pocket and wipes the spit off Larry's face and shirt. Then he gives Larry his handkerchief and pulls Larry's bell-bottoms up by the belt loops in front. "Jesus, man, can't you keep your stupid pants up?"

Larry kicks him hard in the shin, then pushes him away.

Chase looks down at his leg, like it belongs to somebody else. Then he looks back at Larry and limps to the other side of the cable car. He bends over to rub his shin and starts to roll his pants leg up to look at the red scraped welt rising on the skin over the bone, but he changes his mind and lets his arms dangle out the side of the cable car instead. He looks down at the crowds of people, at the rows of seats in the Cotton Bowl, at the rows of cars in the parking lots. His leg throbs, and the people below all look like ants, like the people looked on the sidewalks downtown when he looked down with his father from the roof of the Mobil building.

In a while, the cable car passes over the blue water of a long reflecting pool leading to the exposition center, and Chase shouts out over the wind, "Hey, man, you guys see that go-cart they got down at the Auto Show?" He looks back at Larry over his shoulder.

Larry shakes his head. The handkerchief is wadded in his mouth.

"It's cool as shit," Chase says. "And that car—"

Larry walks up to Chase, pulls the handkerchief out of his mouth, holds it out to him.

"No thanks, man," Chase says. "You keep it."

Larry sits on the cable car's scuffed floor, holds on to his ankles, hugs his knees up against his chest.

"Look," Chase says, folding his arms against the wind, "he's not coming back, all right?"

Larry puts his head between his knees and stares down at the toes of his loafers.

"The man's a jerk. You need to forget about him, okay? All right?"

Larry doesn't look at Chase. He doesn't say anything. He rocks himself.

The cable car bumps over the pulley at the top of the last steel pillar and swings in the wind as the car starts down. Chase looks over the side and watches the shadow of the cable car pass over the roof of the exposition center. He looks back at Larry.

"Listen, man, I got an idea."

Hours later, at 5:30 P.M., long after the school buses have left without them, Chase has already filled out forty sweepstakes forms, and Larry twice that many. Chase stands on a folding metal chair and stuffs all his forms into the slot at the top of the chicken-wire tumbler next to the Shelby Cobra GT. He looks over at the other tumbler and thinks maybe he has time now to fill out a few more forms for the go-cart, maybe one or two for Larry, maybe a few more for himself. Then he sees Larry scribble something onto a blank form and toss it into a pile of forms on the table next to the bandstand.

Chase walks to the table. He picks up one of the sweepstakes forms from Larry's pile, then another form, and another.

Except for the name *Larry*, with the *r*'s reversed, Chase can't read any of the writing. It's all loops and spikes, radio waves, lightning bolts, pigs' tails. He looks at Larry, who's still writing fast, biting his tongue between his teeth.

"Man, what are you *doing?*" Chase holds up one of Larry's forms. "How's somebody supposed to *read* this?"

Larry doesn't look at him. "Don't know," he says. "It's cursive."

Chase grabs the sleeve of Larry's sweatshirt and points to the tumbler. "You didn't put any of these in *there*, did you?"

"Yeah," Larry says.

"How many?"

Larry shrugs free of Chase's grip and lays both hands palm down on his pile of sweepstakes forms. "These many."

"Jesus." Chase sweeps Larry's pile of forms onto the floor, then prints out his mother's name and address on a blank form and holds it out to Larry. "This is how you do it, man. Like this."

Larry looks at the form but doesn't take it. He looks down at the forms scattered all over the floor, kicks at them, stands on them, shuffles his feet in them.

Chase grabs Larry hard by the shoulders. "Look, this is important, you understand? If us two don't get Mom that car, she'll never get out of bed. You want her to get out of bed, don't you?"

"Yeah," Larry says.

"All right, then, here." Chase hands Larry the form. "Just print. And no cursive, all right?"

Larry picks up a blank form and prints out their mother's name and address, copying from the form Chase has already filled out for him, curling his tongue up over his lip, taking his time. The *r*'s are still reversed, but Chase can almost read the writing now.

He looks back at the go-cart for a moment, then at the girl with the shiny legs who can't stop smiling on the rotating auto display. He takes a stubby pencil from the box on the table and starts filling out more forms for the Shelby Cobra GT.

An hour later, Chase shakes the cramp out of his hand and watches as the band tunes up. The fiddle player taps the microphone and blows into it, then hands it over to the bald emcee.

"All right, folks," the emcee says, "just a reminder that the drawing tonight is at seven o'clock. That's just another thirty minutes from now. One other announcement, and then we'll have us some more music." The emcee unfolds a piece of paper he's taken from his coat pocket. "Let's see here, looks like we've got us a couple of missing kids. Chase and Larry Garrett, if you boys are wandering around out there somewhere in the hall, please go to the information booth at the park entrance. The law's been looking all over for you." The bald emcee squints out at the audience, then hands the mike back over to the fiddle player.

Just then, Chase looks over to see a security guard say something into a walkie-talkie and sidestep through the crowd toward Larry. Chase walks to Larry's table and takes him by the sleeve.

"Let's get out of here."

In the public men's room, Chase sits on the cold U-shaped seat with his pants down around his ankles. He ducks down to look under the stall partition between him and Larry, and Larry's feet have disappeared again. Chase pulls his pants up, walks over to the next stall, and opens the stall door. Larry's standing balanced on the rim of the toilet, unrolling the tissue paper from the dispenser and wrapping it around his head like a turban.

"Man, don't you ever *stop*? Get down from there."

Larry starts to step down, but then his foot slips on the ceramic rim, and a moment later he's standing with one foot in the toilet bowl, the clear water up to his ankle, the white paper hanging down over his left eye.

"Just sit," Chase says. "That's all I'm asking you to do. You don't have to go or anything. Just sit down till I tell you to get up, okay?"

"Yeah," Larry says. He pulls his dripping loafer out of the toilet and stomps his shoe on the concrete floor, his foot squelching inside.

After Chase takes a seat on the toilet again, a man opens the plywood door to his stall. The man's long sleeve is folded in half, safetypinned to his armless shoulder, and creased flat at the elbow like it's been ironed. The man looks at Chase a moment, then lets the stall door swing shut. A few minutes later, another man opens the stall door. The skin on his face is knobby like tree bark, pocked and stubbly with wiry black hair. The spring on the stall door sings again, and the door claps shut.

When Chase hears one of the men make a coughing grunt, he

whispers, "Jesus," then stands to pull up his pants and walks to one of the sinks along the wall to wash his hands.

"All right, we can go now," he tells Larry over his shoulder.

He looks up into the long mirror and watches Larry walk down the row of stalls, opening one door after another, letting each one slam shut with a loud pop.

"Cut that out, will you?" Chase says.

Larry doesn't look at him. When he opens the last stall door, he doesn't let it go. He looks inside the stall.

Chase turns the crank on the paper towel dispenser but no paper comes out. He slings the water off his hands, wipes his hands on his trousers, then starts for the exit.

"Come on," he tells Larry. "Let's get going, man."

Larry's still holding open the door to the last stall. His mouth is open a little.

"What?" Chase says. "What are you looking at?"

Just then, the man with the knobby skin looks out past the last stall's open door, and he runs by Chase, out the men's room exit. Then the man with the empty sleeve pinned to his shoulder stumbles out the same stall, his shirttail hanging out, a long white banner of tissue paper stuck to the heel of his shoe and streaming along the floor behind him till it catches in the exit door and the man's gone.

Larry lets go of the stall door and it slaps shut. He looks at Chase. His eyes are big.

"Freak show," he says.

⸻

Chase and Larry shoulder their way through the crowd gathered at the stage.

At one corner of the stage, the fat junior high kid Chase saw earlier watches his father and the security guard each take one end of the go-cart and carry it down the stage steps.

At the opposite corner of the stage, Chase steps up onto one of the stage's two-by-four cross-braces and leans on his elbows against the stage floor. Larry steps up onto the cross-brace next to him.

"They gave the go-cart away," Chase says. "Man, what a load."

"Yeah," Larry says.

Center stage, the bald emcee spins the tumbler, and the sweepstakes forms flutter and fall like white birds in a wire cage. The emcee stops the tumbler, turns it over to unlatch the door at the top, then reaches an arm inside, riffles through the jumble of forms with his hand, then pulls out a form and walks up to the mike.

"All right, folks, the moment you've all been waiting for. The winner of the *all new Shelby Cobra GT convertible* is—" The band's drummer starts a roll on his snare. The emcee squints at the form in his palm, holds it up a little closer, and shakes his head. He hands it over to the fiddle player, who looks at the form, shakes his head, too, then hands it back to the emcee. The emcee gives the drummer a look behind him, and the drum roll stops.

"We're sorry about the delay here, folks, but we're having trouble making out much of this chicken scratching. Must be some kind of practical joke." The emcee holds the form out for the audience to see. "Looks like we'll just have to draw again." The emcee drops the form, which feathers back and forth in the air and settles onto the stage floor.

"Wait," Chase shouts and pulls himself up onto the stage. He starts for the emcee, who's already turning the tumbler again, but Larry has Chase by the ankle.

"Want up," Larry says.

"Stay there," Chase tells him. "Let go of my leg."

Larry shakes his head.

"All right. Okay." Chase takes Larry by the hand and pulls him up onto the stage, then picks up the form the emcee's dropped onto the stage floor. He looks at the writing—all lightning bolts, radio waves, pigs' tails—then steps out in front of the emcee, who's already pulled another form from the tumbler and started for the mike.

"This is my brother's," Chase says, blocking the emcee's way, holding the form up under the emcee's nose. "He's the one that wrote this. He's the one that won that car."

"Yeah," Larry says.

The emcee smiles out at the audience and whispers to Chase, "Listen, son, why don't you and your brother just get down off here? Don't be a pain in the ass." He steps around Chase and Larry and strides up to the mike. He glances at the sweepstakes form he's pulled from the tumbler and starts to speak into the mike again, but this time Chase runs around in front of him and knocks the mike stand to the stage floor.

The microphone bounces, echoing out and feeding back over the public address system. Chase picks up the mike and points over to the Shelby Cobra GT rotating on the auto display next to the stage.

"Listen, man," he tells the audience, hearing his own strange voice boom out all around him, "that car over there belongs to my brother. Really, it's for my mom, but she won't get out of bed."

Just then the emcee snatches the mike from Chase's hand and starts to speak, but before he can say anything Larry's kicked the emcee hard in the shin. The emcee drops the mike onto the stage floor, holds on to his leg, and hops around a while on the stage. Larry picks up the mike and shouts, "Yeah," over the loudspeakers, then hands the mike back over to Chase.

But then the security guard has Chase by the waist, has dragged him down the stage steps, is carrying him upside down through the crowd. All Chase can see are hundreds of feet. All he can hear is the hiss of his own blood spilling down into his head.

"No fair," he shouts out at all the people's feet. "Hey, man, let me down."

In the exposition center's main office, the security guard drops Chase onto the reception room couch. The fiddle player drops Larry next to him and walks out of the room.

"All right," the guard says, "what's you boys' names?"

Chase tells him.

The guard nods his head, then tells Chase he's got a phone call to make and leaves the room.

When the guard comes back, Chase hands him the crumpled sweepstakes form with Larry's scribbling all over it.

"That's our car," Chase says. "They're giving our car away, right now."

The guard looks at the form a while, turns it over a few times, grinning. He leaves the room again, and when he comes back a second time a few minutes later, he hands Chase a red plastic snap-together model of a Shelby Cobra GT convertible.

"It's something anyway," the guard says.

Chase runs his finger along the stick-on racing stripe that runs over the air scoop on the hood of the plastic car. He finds one corner of the decal, peels it back a little, then presses it back down. He hands the model over to Larry, who spins the front wheels, runs the car along the arm of the couch, then gets down on his knees and pushes the car along the linoleum floor.

"We better get going," the guard says.

Outside, it's night already, and Chase sees the lights blinking along the tracks of the Texas Tornado, then hears people scream as their roller coaster car slows at the top of the high tracks and falls down the steep incline. The guard opens the door to his patrol car, waits until Chase and Larry have gotten into the backseat.

"You taking us to prison?" Chase says as the guard turns the car out of the fairgrounds. It's a dumb thing to ask, he knows, the minute he says it.

"Not this time." The guard looks back at Chase for a moment, then looks ahead and turns another corner at the end of the block. "Looks like I'm the only one around who can take you boys home. Your mom says she doesn't have a car."

Chase looks at the guard, but he can't think of anything to say back, the man's so stupid. He glances out the window as the patrol car passes the concrete-block building with the red neon sign that flashes *All Nude Girls. All Nude Girls.* Then he looks up at the billboard of Smiling Joe grinning down at him across the street.

In the backseat next to him, Larry runs the model car over the passenger door, then up and across the window glass.

"Roooom," Larry says.

When the guard's patrol car pulls up next to the curb, their mother is standing in the front yard with her arms folded. She thanks the guard and waves his car off, then points down the street to the Nelsons' willow at the street corner.

"Pick yourselves a green one," she says.

"We won you a car, Mom," Chase says. "Really. But then they took it away."

"Yeah," Larry says.

Their mother takes the model from Larry's hands and points down to the street corner again.

"Now," she says.

Down the street, standing under the willow's dangling branches, Larry holds out a switch he's stripped for Chase to look at. It's only about three inches long.

"Not good enough," Chase says, then hands Larry the one he's stripped for himself. Chase looks back up the street at his mother. Her arms are still folded. Chase reaches up, pulls down another long branch, and breaks it off. It's too stiff and bumpy, but his mother's in a hurry, he knows.

"Let's go," he tells Larry. "Jesus, man."

In the house, their mother leads them down the hall to Larry's room. There aren't any shoes or shirts or trucks on the floor. The bed's been made. Their mother takes Larry by the elbow, leads him up to his closet, points at the black bald spot on the shag rug next to the closet door.

"Who did this?" she asks him.

Larry looks down at his loafers.

She looks at Chase. "Who *did* this?" she asks again.

Chase doesn't say anything.

"You *scared* me," their mother shouts at him all of a sudden, and Chase jumps in his shoes. She waits a moment, breathes out a long sigh, then shouts at Larry, "I thought something might've *happened* to you."

Chase and Larry stand there a while, say nothing, wait.

"All right," she says, "drop your drawers."

After Chase has stepped out of his skivvies, he grips the switch in his wet fist and stands on his toes a little, thinking about the switch against his ankles. He looks down at himself, hoping she doesn't hit him *there*. Then he looks back at his mother, holds his switch out for her to take.

"No," she says.

She picks up the wastepaper basket next to Larry's dresser and holds it out in front of Chase.

He looks at her, then down at the wastebasket, and drops his switch inside. He stoops to pick up his skivvies and trousers, steps into them before she can change her mind again.

She holds the basket out for Larry, and he drops his switch in, too. Then she says, "Hold your arms up," and she helps Larry pull his sweatshirt over his head. "Now, take these nasty jeans to the utility room," she tells him. "Now."

Larry picks up his muddy bell-bottoms and runs naked out of his room. Their mother puts the Shelby Cobra GT model on top of Larry's dresser. She looks at Chase.

"I've not been very—" she says but doesn't finish. "I bet you're hungry," she says. "Listen, are you hungry?"

Thirty minutes later, Chase walks by Larry's room and sees Larry standing by his dresser, looking at the plastic photo I.D. their father used to clip onto his shirt pocket each morning before he went to work.

In the kitchen down the hall, their mother is pan-frying pork chops, sitting on a barstool next to the stove, talking to somebody on the phone. "No, Jacob," she says, "I don't *need* a restraining order. I need my car. The bastard took my *car*."

When Larry sees Chase watching him from the hallway, Chase walks into his room, picks up the wastepaper basket next to Larry's dresser, and holds it out.

Larry looks a moment at the two switches sticking out of the basket, then drops the I.D. inside. Then he takes his Creature from the Black Lagoon model down from his dresser and shakes it in front of Chase's nose.

"Arrgggghhh," Larry says.

Chase takes the Shelby Cobra GT model down from Larry's dresser, turns it over a few times to look at it, then puts it back up.

He sits lopsided on Larry's bed, stands back up to look at what he's sat on but sees nothing there on the bedspread. Then he reaches back into his hip pocket and takes out the plastic monkey he won at the fair. Its belly is smashed in a little, but otherwise it looks all right.

He stands the monkey up in the front seat of the Shelby Cobra GT model on Larry's dresser, stands back to look at it. "I wonder if this stupid thing really smokes." Chase pulls out one of the pin-sized cigarettes taped to the monkey's backside and sticks it into the monkey's mouth.

He and Larry both wait, but no smoke comes out.

"Man, what a load," Chase says.

"Yeah," Larry says.

Chase looks at his brother. "Anyway, least she didn't whack us."

"Yeah."

"Least she got out of bed."

"Yeah," Larry says. At that moment, the monkey blows out a tiny puff of smoke.

A Discussion
of Property

Jenkins and Rorick had agreed to start hunting at
5 A.M., but Jenkins punched out two hours early at the textile mill so
he could get back home to Dawna by three. That would give him and
her a little time, he thought, maybe. When Jenkins got home,
though, Rorick's old GMC was already parked in the peach orchard
out front and the truck's hood was cold. Jenkins walked the clay driveway around back. At first he thought he heard the whippoorwills
calling, but it was too early, too cold. Then he saw that Rorick had
Dawna bent over the new deep freeze on the back porch.

"Jesus God Almighty," he tried to say, but it came out more like
"Jesus got all muddy."

Which was sufficient. Rorick heard and backed away from Dawna and pulled up his Lees. Dawna slid off the freezer top, smoothed down her long Crimson Tide T-shirt, which she always wore to bed, and padded barefoot across the porch, into the house.

Rorick shoved his hands far down into his pants pockets and kept them there, but he looked at Jenkins straight on from over the porch rail.

"You and me, we spent half a month's pay apiece for that deep freeze," Jenkins said. "It's the best we could buy in Loachapoka, and now it's ruint for me." His breath hung like a torn rag in front of his face. The stars overhead were buckshot holes through a barn loft.

Rorick said nothing.

Jenkins walked up the steps, which sagged to one side and yawned under his weight. "Zip up your britches," he said, then stepped past Rorick into his house, stopping the screened door with his heel so it wouldn't slap into the frame. The mounted heads of two bucks he and Rorick had shot the year before stared down at him from over the kitchen table, glass-eyed, grinning.

In the bedroom he pulled his thirty-aught-six down from the top shelf of his closet, then laid the case at the foot of the bed, next to Dawna, and opened it. He pulled a pair of long johns from the bottom drawer and undressed, the last time, he supposed, in front of his wife. He stepped into the legs of the camouflage hunting suit he wore over his long johns, slipped his arms through the sleeves, and zipped up the front. Then he took two boxes of shells from the top drawer of his dresser, dropped them into his gun case, and snapped it shut.

Dawna was chewing the polish off her thumbnail.

"What is this?" he said. "You think I'm going to shoot you?"

She shook her head, but he didn't believe her anymore.

"Look," he said, "Rorick and me, we'll be back about noon. I want you and your shit out of here by then. You can have the Trans Am."

He picked up his gun case, walked around to the back door, and opened it. Rorick still stood outside next to the porch rail, not leaning against it, his hands far down into his pockets, to his knees, it seemed like.

"We'll have to take your GMC," Jenkins told Rorick. "We going, or not?"

"You're fucking with me, right?" Rorick said.

"That's not what it looks like to me," Jenkins said. "Your truck," he said and nudged Rorick with his gun case. "We're going hunting."

They walked the fence line for twenty minutes, Jenkins with his back to Rorick. He wasn't thinking about Rorick now, only about the way the sky grayed over the tree line behind the stubble of a soybean field. Jenkins stopped at a twisted cedar post, to cross over. Rorick tucked his thirty-thirty under his arm and held his hand out for Jenkins' rifle, and Jenkins handed it over to him. Rorick leaned the rifles against the post, stepped on the bottom wire, and held the top wire up while Jenkins ducked through, then past, the barbs. Rorick handed the rifles over the fence and ducked through himself.

Jenkins laid his rifle and Rorick's at the roots of a stunted blackjack oak and faced Rorick as he turned from the fence. He waited until Rorick was ready, then threw a quick knuckle-jab at the bridge of Rorick's nose. A loud pop echoed out over the rutted fields. Rorick wobbled on his heels a little but straightened again. Then he hit Jenkins in the throat, throwing his other fist up into Jenkins' chin in two quick sweeps.

They looked at each other a while. Rorick blinked and made a fist over his nose. Jenkins heard the sputtering whine of a chainsaw far off, and he tried to swallow. Then he and Rorick were both on the ground.

When two crows flew overhead and called out *Dawna, Dawna,* Jenkins and Rorick stood and dusted themselves off. Jenkins' shirt pocket was torn halfway down, flapping in the cold wind. He tore the rest of it off and handed it to Rorick, who used it to dab at the bubble of blood in his nostril. Jenkins waited, handed Rorick his gun, and hefted his own. They walked on together.

The two deer stands were twenty feet up in two tall pines, a hundred yards apart, across a green clearing from each other. Jenkins sat in one stand and, with his scope, sighted in Rorick, who sat in the other.

They'd built both stands together and sowed winter wheat in the clearing one day the August before. They'd drunk a fifth of Old Crow and woken in the middle of the clearing the next morning without hangovers, their shirts wet with dew. Then they'd both gone home to their own wives. Now they watched each other through cross-hairs.

Jenkins lifted his rifle barrel slowly, sighting in blurred branches and clumps of pine needles. Then he saw a moving gray patch, a mourning dove tucking its wings in and cooing on a limb ten feet above Rorick's head. He squeezed off and watched the explosion of feathers, which floated down in a fine red mist and settled onto Rorick's shoulders and hair.

"Why don't you just shoot me?" Rorick shouted.

Jenkins shot again, dropping an overhead branch into Rorick's lap, then aimed his rifle up at the low clouds and squeezed off three hip shots.

"Dammit, Jenkins, it was just something that happened. It wasn't nothing we planned on."

We, Jenkins thought. Then he couldn't think. He said nothing. He waited for the shots' echoes and Rorick's voice to die in the wind.

No deer had been in the clearing all morning. In a while, he thought he could hear antlers scrape against bark in the distance.

The rifle barrel's bluing tasted like well water in a tin cup. Jenkins tongued the smooth round barrel hole and pulled the rifle stock in closer between his knees, pressing the barrel's mouth up hard against the roof of his own mouth, thumbing the trigger's curve. Then he heard leaf-shuffle at the foot of the tree, and he pulled the rifle barrel out of his mouth. He'd had it there a while, and nothing had happened, nothing would. He sat forward in the stand and made ready.

"Rorick?" someone shouted. Then he heard his own name.

It was Dawna. She walked to the foot of the tree, her white Tide T-shirt tucked into her baggy jeans.

Jenkins aimed his rifle away. "What you doing here?"

"I was afraid."

"Ought to be. You'll get yourself shot coming out here."

She looked up at him and said, "You always talk down to me, that's my main complaint. Either that, or you don't talk to me at all." She cupped her hands over her mouth and shouted, "Rorick?"

"He's in the other stand," Jenkins said. "He's asleep."

She hugged herself bare-armed in the cold, her breasts pressing against the faded red elephant on her T-shirt.

"I don't believe you," she said.

He laughed. Then he felt sick. "I'm sorry I haven't been who you've wanted me to be," he said, then laid his gun on the plywood floor of the stand and climbed down the pine's two-by-four steps, leading her by the arm across the green to the other stand.

"You better not've done nothing to him," she said, shrugging free from his grip at the foot of the other pine. "We both did what we did, but mostly it was my doing."

We, Jenkins thought again. Then he couldn't think at all.

"Rorick," he called up into the pine's canopy, "my wife wants you."

Rorick climbed down from his stand. Dawna saw the cuts on his face and said, "You all right?"

Rorick looked over at Jenkins.

She touched the base of Rorick's nose, where his eyes were purpling and swelling, and he turned his head, away from her. He kept his arms at his sides, his hands in his pockets.

He said, "You shouldn't be here."

"I want you to come back with me," she said. "Something could happen."

"It would've happened by now if it was going to. We're hunting now."

She looked at Jenkins and said, "I'll be down at my sister's."

Jenkins watched her walk back through the high grass into the clearing, her hands in her back pockets, palms out, her thumbs hooked over the back of her baggy jeans. He watched Rorick watch her, then turn away. He felt the bruised knot bulging at his windpipe. He tried to swallow.

Soon she was out of sight, and he told Rorick, "Not much luck here. What you say we try down at the river bottom?"

They waited under a wild terrace of dead kudzu vines that looped and draped over two stooped oaks. Fresh pronged tracks in the mud had led them there to a furrowed pile of dry grass in the shadows, where two deer had slept the night. Jenkins and Rorick sat with their backs to the trees, their rifles at their feet. They said nothing for two hours.

Jenkins hadn't been able to think before, but now he couldn't stop thinking.

Mainly, he thought about the poker games he and Dawna and Rorick and Rorick's wife, Becca, had played Friday nights for over a year. He tried to remember signs he might've missed, the way they might've looked at each other over the card table's green felt, over their fanned cards. Their grins, their little nods.

"You want another beer?" Dawna might've asked Rorick, and it might've meant anything. And the two of them might've stood up and pulled their chairs out from the card table to go to the kitchen together, out to the back porch, innocent enough, just for a minute or two.

And it might've been longer than a minute. Jenkins couldn't remember, it might've been five or ten. He and Becca might've sat there at the card table, staring at each other, making small talk, looking down at their folded hands. And anything might've happened.

Jenkins watched Rorick lean back against the pine, fighting off sleep, his eyes heavy-lidded, his head nodding.

"What you going to tell Becca?" Jenkins said. "You *are* going to tell her, right?"

Rorick straightened. He opened his eyes. "What?"

"You got to tell her, she's got a right. You got to go home and be straight with her, that's my advice to you."

Rorick was quiet. He looked out to the slope down to the Sougahatchee River, where the morning mist was burning off. He was awake now.

"Don't be telling me what to do with my wife."

"And not with *my* wife either, right?" Jenkins said. "Look, this is it, the end of it. I mean, we're not going to shoot nothing today, not now, not in a hundred years. It'll be noon in a while, and you'll have to go home empty-handed and tell Becca you been fucking my wife. Then it'll all be over, and then you and my wife can keep on fucking each other."

"Let it alone," Rorick said.

"Do you love my wife?" Jenkins said. "I mean, have you loved her a long time? What I mean is, I'd like to know if you've got as much love in you as you've got gall. I've got a right."

"Stop it, man," Rorick said.

"Or've you just been fucking her because she's my wife and she's been easy because things've been hard for me and her lately, that's what I'd like to know. Was she easy?"

"Shut up."

"She looked easy enough to me. You could've been anybody, any Joe she saw walking down any road in Loachapoka, and she would've gone for you because she wanted out with me, and you just happened to be around, just happened to be a good excuse for her getting out, am I right?"

"Shut your mouth," Rorick said, gripping his rifle stock and standing in the shadows, pointing his rifle at Jenkins from the hip. "I could kill you, you know that?"

"You already killed me, friend. I been in my rut and you been in yours. My wife's been looking for a way out and you showed her a way. I loved her and you were my friend, and now you're not and now you can have her. The hell with it, it's over."

"Look," Rorick said. "There. Over there."

Jenkins looked at Rorick a long time, then back over his own shoulder.

A buck stood at the slope down to the river.

No, there were two bucks, Jenkins thought.

Rorick raised his rifle to shoot, but Jenkins gripped the rifle barrel, turned it away from the river, and said, "Wait."

"You want this one?" Rorick said. "All right, this one's yours, it's all yours. You can have this one."

"No," Jenkins said, hefting his own rifle and sighting it in. "Look again, but don't shoot."

In his sights, Jenkins saw a buck, then tangled antlers, then the head and neck of another buck, a decaying half-carcass ending at the shoulder, stiff black meat like jerky covered with flies, white spine and ribs sticking through rotted meat and ratted fur, a dead buck's head hanging from the live buck's head.

"Jesus, do you see that, look at that," Rorick said. "Jesus."

Jenkins watched the buck, its head down, dragging the carcass down to the river's edge, into the water. Skin and fur, like a balding rug, stretched over the buck's sharp-boned flanks and ribs. The buck hadn't been able to eat or drink in a long time, and it stumbled into the water and fell, its antlers locked underwater with the dead buck's antlers. The buck struggled to stand.

"It's drowning trying to drink," Jenkins said, and he ran, Rorick following him, down the slope to the river.

Rorick shot first, and Jenkins shouted, "Don't, goddammit."

Then Rorick said, "Shoot for the antlers," and Jenkins understood. He raised his rifle to his shoulder, aimed at the tangled antlers, and shot, the flying bits of shattered antler pelting the water, until his rifle's magazine was empty.

The buck stood from the water, antlerless, its head still down, until it shook its head and saw the other buck's carcass floating free in the water. It lifted its head and looked at Jenkins, then at Rorick, blinking, blowing spray out its nostrils, huffing. Then it shook its head again, slinging an arc of water out from its neck, and it bounded off, arching its back and kicking up water, up to the shore, up into the cover of scrub oak and pine along the shore.

"Jesus," Rorick said. "Jesus, did you see that?"

"Yeah," Jenkins said. "It was something."

They both stood a long time looking down at the carcass floating in the water, down at the ripples of the waves the buck had made.

"Would've made a damn fine trophy," Rorick said.

"A freak trophy," Jenkins said. "Something for people to gawk at."

"It wouldn't've been cheap to mount, but it would've been worth a million bucks."

"Not worth a damn," Jenkins said. "Not worth nothing. A man who'd pay good money for a mount like that wouldn't be worth nothing himself. No damn good, a man like that."

Jenkins and Rorick walked the logging road together, carrying their rifles back to Rorick's truck, arguing about the only buck they'd ever shot at to miss.

Rorick unlocked his door, threw his keys over to Jenkins across the roof of the cab, then opened his own door, and folded his arms at the top of the cab.

"I guess maybe you're right about that buck," he said. "But everything you said before the buck, everything about Dawna and me, you got wrong. What happened was just what happened, and it's only happened this once. You don't got to believe me, I guess. I don't blame you if you don't, but that's the way it is."

"Let's don't talk about it no more," Jenkins said, tossing the keys back to Rorick, and they both got into the truck and drove off together.

When the truck pulled into the peach orchard, the Trans Am Jenkins had driven home early that morning was still parked out front. Rorick turned his truck down the humped clay drive by the house, and Jenkins saw Dawna rocking in her glider next to the deep freeze on the back porch.

Rorick stayed in the truck, his engine still running.

Jenkins got out of the truck and walked over to the porch.

Dawna had changed her clothes. She wore the dress she'd finished on her Singer the day before, the same pattern and flowered cloth she'd bought at the Hancock's in Montgomery.

"I thought you said you'd be down at your sister's," Jenkins said, his foot on the first porch step.

"Well, I changed my mind," she said, rocking.

"I thought I told you to be out of here by now," he said.

"Well, I'm not."

Jenkins looked down at his boot, at the wood's knotted pattern under his heel on the porch step, then at the mud on the heel of his boot.

"I did you wrong," Dawna said, "I know that, but I'm not leaving till you and me talk."

"Nothing to talk about," he said.

"I don't know," she said. "Maybe there's been too much need for talking and not enough talking. Maybe that's been the problem."

"The problem is you expect too much. You expect me to look at you and talk to you after I saw what I saw this morning. You expect more than a man can bear. You expect too goddamn much."

"I know," she said.

Jenkins looked out to Rorick's old GMC. The engine was still running. Rorick's arms were folded over the steering wheel, and his head lay on his arms. He looked to be asleep.

"Hold on a minute," Jenkins said, then scraped the mud from his boot on the corner of the porch step and walked out to Rorick's truck.

Jenkins fanned his hands back, guiding Rorick in as he backed his truck up to the back porch.

"A little to the left," Jenkins shouted. "That's good."

They lifted the deep freeze they'd bought together to keep the venison they'd kill, and they crossed out from the porch steps, stepping up and onto the tailgate. The truck's leaf springs creaked, and the deep freeze was heavy, heavier than Jenkins remembered, and he held it and lifted it and laid his end down in the bed of the truck.

Rorick slammed his truck door shut, and Jenkins told him, "You keep it a while. I don't have much use for it right now, you understand."

"Sure," Rorick said. Then Rorick was driving off, not looking around, out the clay drive around to the front, to the dirt road through the peach orchard, then out to the county road down to Loachapoka.

Jenkins stood on the back porch, his arms folded, and Dawna sat on the glider, rocking. They both looked out at the naked trees and said nothing. It was quiet, too quiet, and Jenkins couldn't think of what to say.

Then he turned to her and said, "Almost got us a buck, a fourteen-pointer, at least," and she stopped rocking. "You wouldn't believe what a fix it'd gotten itself into."

It was the only way he could think to begin.

Hoot's
Last
Bubble
Bath

For Timothy Jefferson Akers, the better storyteller

"Heartbreak? You want to know about heartbreak?" says my great uncle, Thomas "Hoot" Ponder.

We're both drinking Jim Beam and tap water at his breakfast table and he's talking about what it's meant to be a certified public accountant for the last fifty years, and then all of a sudden he starts in. I never know from one minute to the next what'll trigger it all, but drinking helps and I can always hope and now I'm happy. I'm a happy man when he starts in.

"No," I say, "I don't want to hear about it."

"Well, I can tell you all about it," Hoot says anyway. "I can tell you everything you need to know."

I wait, even though I can't.

"This," Hoot says. "You and me coming to this. A young man drinking night after night with an old man, when he could be out drinking with a pretty girl. Goddamn, I love a pretty girl." Hoot lifts his glass in a toast to the pretty girls of the world and takes a sip. The ice in his glass is all melted, but he smiles and leans toward me. "This. Two men not having the dignity and good sense to keep it to themselves. This. Two men talking like this."

I lean toward him and say, "I haven't said a word." I smile. I take a drink. I'm happier than I've been in a while.

"This," Hoot says, "is heartbreak."

———

Hoot's wife, my great aunt Libby, is dying in the bedroom down the hall. She's eighty-nine, fifteen years older than Hoot. A few months back, her vertigo got worse, and one morning she slipped in the bathtub and shattered her hip. A week later, after my divorce was final, I moved back home to Dallas and I heard the bad news. I called my great uncle to offer my sympathy. Nothing like a divorce to make a man have sympathy.

"Why don't you come on over?" Hoot said. His voice sounded like trying to force gravel through a coffee filter. "We could talk, the two of us, maybe have us a few drinks."

"I don't know," I said.

I wasn't comfortable with the idea of coming over. I hadn't seen Hoot since I was a kid. My father had made me and my mother and my three sisters dress up and go to Hoot's house every Christmas Day I can remember since I was ten. Then he and my father had a big falling out because he wouldn't loan my father any more money. Hoot and I'd already said more to each other over the phone than we'd ever said all the times I'd visited him growing up.

"Maybe I'll drop by," I said, "but just for a little while. I got some laundry to do."

"Do it here."

"I don't know," I said.

Hoot's house on Mercedes was still covered with English ivy, and the lawn still looked like a putting green, even though the grass hadn't been cut in a month or so. When I drove up the driveway, the grass on the center hump brushed up against the underside of my seventy-six Volare, and Hoot leaned out the door of his screened-in sleeping porch.

"Goddamn, Travis," he shouted, "you've grown."

"I hope so," I shouted back. "I'll be thirty-one next month." I pulled four Glad bags of laundry out of the backseat and walked up the sidewalk.

"Well, I'm a stupid son of a bitch," he said, then held the screened door open for me. "Come on in."

Hoot and Libby's living room hadn't changed any that I could tell, even after twenty years. The white Steinway grand piano still angled into one corner beside two Louis the Fourteenth armchairs, and two white ceramic ballerinas still danced on the fireplace mantel. Except for a thick layer of dust on everything, it all still showed Libby's touch.

When I was a kid, Libby'd always been beautiful and elegant, a smart woman with good taste, except for her taste in men. Christmas Day, I'd listened many times to Libby play Debussy while my sisters fidgeted in the stiff white dresses they'd worn to midnight mass at St. Edward's the night before, while Hoot and my father sat at the breakfast table behind the closed kitchen door, shouting and drinking and cursing and telling dirty jokes.

Hoot led me back to the utility room. It smelled like an overripe diaper hamper, and clothes were scattered in piles all over the floor.

"There's some Cheer around here someplace," he said, then kicked at the piles of clothes a while till there was a clear space on the floor. "Hell, just set your gear down here for now. I told Libby you were coming. She'd like to see you."

In their bedroom, Hoot propped Libby's head up on a lacy pillow and gave her a sip of ice water from a kinked straw. Her face was skull-shadowed, and the veins on her thin hands were like earthworms under waxed paper. It hadn't occurred to me that she could be so old, that she wouldn't be beautiful anymore.

"I hear you're married now," Libby said.

"Not anymore."

"I'm sorry?" she said.

Hoot frowned at me. His look told me that her apology was for not hearing me, and I was glad for the second chance.

"Happily," I said louder.

She smiled. "Tell me her name."

"Stephanie."

"Stephanie, yes, a nice name," she said. "And she's got herself a handsome man. You look so much like Thomas when we were first married." Libby covered her mouth and coughed. "You should bring Stephanie over sometime. Right now, though, I'm a little tired."

In the kitchen, Hoot fixed us both a drink—three or four cubes of ice, a jigger or two of water, the rest Jim Beam. The dishes piled in the sink behind him were starting to mold over, and overturned cans of Campbell's cream of chicken soup were scattered all over the countertop. It all looked a little too familiar, like the kitchen in my East Dallas efficiency. When I took a swallow from my drink, my throat clamped shut.

I walked to the sink and stoppered it, then turned on the kitchen faucet, squirting Ivory into the steamy water and rinsing off a rusty Brillo pad.

"Don't, Travis," Hoot said.

"Why don't you just sit down," I said.

He paced back and forth across the kitchen and didn't say anything for a while. Then he started in: "My Libby Fay's been to the hospital four times in the last two months, and the orthopedic surgeons at Baylor have cut on her twice. They haven't got the balls to admit her hip won't ever mend, but they'll take my money to cut on her again, if I let them. Doctors. Sons of bitches."

"Sit down," I said. "Take it easy."

Hoot kept pacing. The white stubble on his face was almost a beard, and he'd been wearing the same clothes for days. I hadn't really paid much attention before, but he was drunk—soused, really—and he hadn't eaten or bathed in a while, I could see that now.

"I retired early so Libby and I could spend some time together," he

said. "We were going to vacation in Hawaii first, take some Norwe-
gian cruise ship for three or four days, then spend a week in Maui.
Libby'd already made the reservations. We were going to get *lei*-ed,
I told her, and she wasn't offended by this dirty old man, by all his
nonsense. She stood up in the bathtub and laughed at my bad joke
and asked me for a bath towel. I left the bathroom for maybe half a
second to get a dry towel from the hall closet and then, just like that,
our lives were over."

Hoot stopped pacing and looked out the kitchen window for a
while. "I need to cut the yard," he said. "I need to wash Libby's
things. I need to do Judd Archer's taxes. I need to brush my goddamn
teeth." He looked at me over his shoulder. "Things are going to hell
around here, you don't have to tell me."

I kept scrubbing. I didn't say a word.

Then Hoot bumped me with his rear end and said, "Scootch over.
I'll wash and you dry. Dish towels are in the hall closet. I'd go get
you one myself, but—" Hoot just looked at me a moment and somehow I understood.

That night, we did Libby's laundry. The next night, we did Hoot's.
I didn't get around to my own for another week, but I was happy
enough.

One morning a week or so later, my phone rang at 5 A.M.

"Get that, will you, Steph?" I said.

I turned on the lamp and saw the travel alarm I'd just bought at
Target, the old chest of drawers I'd just taken down from my mom's
attic, the lamp and the lamp table and the daybed I'd bought at the
Garland Road Goodwill.

Stephanie wasn't there in my bed, I could see that. She was sleeping in another bed, completely apart from my life now, in another
city a long way off, and I'd probably never see her again. Hoot was
on the phone.

"What's wrong?" I said.

"Libby won't let me touch her," he said. "She doesn't know who
I am."

"I know what you mean," I wanted to say. But didn't. "I'll be right
over," I said.

When Hoot opened his front door, I could hear Libby shouting from the bedroom.

"She can't make it to the bathroom by herself anymore, and she won't let me help her," Hoot said, wearing just his ratty skivvies and house shoes, his white-haired belly and floppy breasts bouncing as he paced across the living room. "She just messed herself and she won't let me anywhere near her." Hoot's thick white eyebrows stuck out like horns. He looked a little crazy.

"'I have to clean you up, honey,' I told her. I said, 'Honey, you've messed yourself, and I have to clean you up.' She was shouting at me, Travis, and she's never shouted at me before in her entire life. I pulled back the sheets and pulled up her nightgown and tried to sponge her clean. Then she hit me. I swear, she balled up her little fist and hauled off and knocked the Jesus out of me." Hoot pointed at the swelling bruise under his eye. "She hit me here, right here. Then she said, 'Shit.' She shouted at me and said, 'Who are you? Shit. Get your hands off me. Son of a bitch.'"

"Did you call a doctor?" I said. "You should call a doctor."

"I never in my life heard her say such things, Travis," he kept on. "They're not in her vocabulary. Before now, I did all the foul-mouthing around here. Libby wouldn't've said *shit* if she'd had a mouthful."

"God," I said.

"I'm telling you, Travis, that woman in there, I don't know who she is. That's not my Libby Fay in there."

"You call a doctor," I said. "And get some clothes on. I'll check to see if she's okay."

In the bedroom, Libby tried to sit up when she saw me. She'd been crying. "Thomas," she said, "where have you been? Thomas, there's a man in our house."

I looked for Hoot behind me in the doorway, but he wasn't there. She was talking to me, I could see that.

"Aunt Libby," I said, "it's me, Travis."

"Honey," she said, "I'm so glad you're home. That man, he was a communist. He wanted to steal all our mail."

I held her and tried to get her to lie flat. I said, "Everything's going to be all right, Libby. I'll be right back."

When I ran back to the kitchen, Hoot said, "I went ahead and called Harry Barlow. He hasn't made a house call in thirty goddamn years and he's been retired for almost that long, but he said he'd be right over." Hoot started down the hall toward Libby's bedroom.

"Wait," I said, stopping him.

"*Senile dementia*, that's what they called it in the old days," Dr. Barlow explained after he'd examined Aunt Libby. She was quiet now. Dr. Barlow was stooped over and at least as old as Libby, and he kept taking his thick wire-rims off and wiping them with his shirt-tail. "A stroke, most likely," he said, "either that or Alzheimer's. Maybe both. Right now, your wife's disoriented, and she seems to be having herself some kind of psychotic episode. There's no telling how long that might last, Tom, and there's a chance it might be perma-nent. She's also got herself a bad case of infected bedsores, and she's got two broken fingers, from hitting you, I suppose. And there's her hip, of course. None of this looks too good. If I didn't know you better, Tom, I'd report you for neglect."

"This is terrible," Hoot said. "Libby Fay."

"What should we do?" I asked Dr. Barlow.

"Right now, she needs a disinfectant sponge bath before the am-bulance gets here. I've already admitted her to Baylor. Meantime, Tom, you should arrange to get Libby into a nursing home."

"No, sir," Hoot said, "I will *not* put her into one of those places."

"Then you'll need to get her a day nurse," Dr. Barlow said. "A good one. Libby'll most likely be bedridden for the rest of her life, but she's not getting the kind of care she needs around here." Dr. Barlow squinted at Hoot accusingly, then put his glasses on and tucked his shirttail back in. "Right now, I could use some help with Libby. The ambulance should be here anytime now."

"She won't have anything to do with me," Hoot said, his head down.

"She thinks he's a communist," I said. "She thinks I'm him."

Hoot looked at me. "Doc Barlow needs your help. I need your help. Libby needs your help. Will you be me for a while?"

"For a while," I said, and I followed Dr. Barlow back to Libby's bedroom.

The next day, I moved my gear into one of Hoot's guest bedrooms, thinking I'd be there maybe a week or two at most. He said he wanted to pay me for my help, but I told him I wasn't interested. Then he insisted on feeding me and paying the rent for my efficiency till he found Libby a day nurse, till I found myself a job. It's been over two months since then, and I still haven't gone anywhere.

"Heartbreak," Hoot says and raises his glass.

"They called Libby a cradle robber when she married me in 1935," he says, "but I called her my turn-of-the-century girl. She turned thirty-five on New Year's Day the day we married, and she was a beauty, a real gentlewoman, I can tell you. I was hung over and twenty and a goddamn fool. Now she's robbed the cradle again."

Hoot's talking about me, of course.

Aunt Libby's been back home from the hospital now for over a month, and the second day nurse Hoot hired isn't working out. She feeds Libby and turns her every three hours to try to heal the bedsores, but every time Libby sees the nurse, she shouts, *Bitch*! Every time she sees Hoot, she screams. She won't talk to anyone but me, and with me, she's always polite. Since the morning she went to the hospital, Hoot hasn't been able to see or talk to his wife of over fifty years.

"For about the fourth or fifth time in my life, I can't remember which," Hoot starts in, "I've come to the conclusion that my life is over." He weaves a little bit at the breakfast table, trying to get me into focus.

"The first time I thought my life was over," he says, "was when the local abortionist's daughter ran off with Vance Villastrego, my third cousin, the son of a bitch. I won't get into that."

"Please do," I say.

"I'm telling this. Don't get me off the point."

"What's the point?"

"Hell, I don't know."

"Go ahead," I say.

"The second time I thought my life was over," he says, "was when

I met Libby Lafayette Jackson at the Lone Star Gas Company, and it was all a little bit too much like right now. She absolutely refused to have a thing to do with me. I was doing the company taxes, and she was the secretary for the vice-president, and every time I drove down to Oak Cliff to turn in the monthly ledger, I left flowers on her desk. A single-stem yellow rose one February, bluebonnets I'd picked myself out in Waxahachie the next May. She was a lady, I could tell."

"That's sweet," I say.

"Oh, shut up," Hoot says, "and let me tell it.

"'I have thirty-seven wildflower allergies,' Libby told me. 'You're only a child,' she said.

"To make a long goddamn story short, Travis, she finally agreed to a proper courtship and we fell in love, all that, and she had a fight with her mother and a falling out with her father, but she said she'd marry me anyway. Then, wouldn't you know it, we took the streetcar downtown to get the blood test for our marriage license, and they told me I had TB. I wrote Libby a long poem about dying for love, and I broke off our engagement. Then I packed two changes of clothes and a sputum cup and hitchhiked to the place they called Lungerville, the Texas State Tuberculosis Sanatorium, just west of San Angelo. That was the third time I thought my life was over.

"The fourth time," Hoots says, "well, hell, I never told anybody about the fourth time."

"Not even Libby?" I say.

"No, sir. *Never.*"

"Why not?"

"It would've killed her. She would've killed *me.*"

"You can tell me," I say. "What was her name?"

"Arna. Arna Harkness. What the hell."

"Go ahead," I say. "This is in strictest confidence."

"Arna Harkness was the half-Cherokee daughter of an Oklahoma bootlegger, and she was one of those TB nurses you might've heard about. She had the reputation for being a fine, caring nurse on the ward and for knowing how to have herself a fine time afterward. She had TB herself, of course, a mild case like mine, and she thought she was going to die. All the time she was walking up and down the ward, coughing and saying crazy things like, 'Before I die, I want to run naked in the rain.'

"To make another long goddamn story short, Travis, I got to know Arna Harkness pretty well. One night after it'd been raining for two weeks straight, Arna smuggled us a jar of her daddy's best clear corn whiskey, and I stole an old Willy's jeep that belonged to the sanatorium director. She and I drove out to the gravel pits and drank us some moonshine. Then we threw the jeep's canvas top down and threw off all our clothes and drove naked up and down old state Highway 87 half the night in the pouring rain. I've had a feeling for years it was the best night of my life, but that's mainly conjecture. I still can't remember a damn thing that happened."

"You're making all this up," I say.

"No, sir," Hoot says. "Now, shut up, I'm not finished yet.

"The long and short of it is, that was the first and last goddamn time I ever went running around buck naked in the rain. It didn't do either me or Arna Harkness a bit of good. Almost killed us both, in fact. I was the lucky one. They made me stay flat on my back outside during one of the worst West Texas winters on record. I stayed bundled up with ten army blankets over me and hot oven bricks at my feet on one of those sleeping porches like Libby and I built on to the front of this house back in forty-eight. But Arna Harkness had it worse. They put her in the goners' barracks, on the artificial pneumothorax, collapsed one of her lungs, the whole awful goddamn business. Hell, I thought we both were going to die, so I wrote up a poem for Arna Harkness and asked her to marry me right away. She never wrote me back, though. I never saw her again after that."

"She died?" I say.

"No, hell, no," Hoot says. "She just didn't want to marry me or see me again, that's all."

"Then how do you know she didn't die?"

"I just know. She's been a nurse over at Parkland Hospital for years, was one of the attending nurses when Kennedy got shot back in sixty-three, lives about fifteen miles from here on Beltline Road in Plano."

"How do you know all this?" I say. "You been checking up on her? You two been having little secret liaisons all these years?"

"No, Travis, hell, no," he says. "I just read the *Times Herald*, is all. Her number's in the phone book, so call her up for all I care. She'd probably deny knowing me. Anyway, that was all over fifty years ago, the fourth time I thought my life was over.

"The fifth time," Hoot says, "well, I guess I'm working on the fifth time right now."

"Well, I called her," I tell Hoot a few days later.

Libby's shouting at the fourth day nurse down the hall, using profanity even Hoot would be ashamed of. We've had a string of awful luck with day nurses. The last two refused to do housework, and then Hoot refused and now I've refused. The dishes are piling up and molding over in the kitchen sink again.

"Called who?" Hoot shouts over Libby's shouts, then takes a big swallow of his Jim Beam. He's still wearing the same ratty T-shirt he's worn all week. It's gauze-thin in places and covered with holes shaped like little spinning galaxies. Sometimes I've seen him wash his face and underarms with Ivory liquid in the kitchen sink, but that's the closest he's come to doing the dishes or taking a bath, either one, so far as I can tell. Trying to take care of him and Libby has lost some of its romance, I got to admit.

"Arna Harkness," I say. "I called her."

For a moment my words don't register. Then Hoot's eyes get big and his mouth opens, but he can't say anything. I expected a reaction, of course.

Hoot stands from his chair and leans on the breakfast table. "You did _what?_"

"I called Arna Harkness. Libby needs a nurse, and Arna Harkness has been a nurse for over fifty years. You said so yourself. Made sense to me."

Hoot says nothing, so I go on.

"When I called, she said, yes, of course she remembered Tom Ponder, how could she forget, she'd be glad to help out. She retired two years ago, and she said she could always use the extra money. I tried to set up an interview with her here tomorrow afternoon, but she said, no, she had her low-impact aerobics at five and her Al-Anon at eight, but she said she could probably squeeze us in sometime tomorrow evening around seven. So I said that's fine. Seemed like a nice enough lady to me."

"Are you absolutely goddamn out of your mind?" Hoot says, quietly. He's not shouting, which is encouraging.

"Seemed like a good idea to me at the time," I say. I'm smiling just a little, I admit it.

"No," Hoot says. He walks to the kitchen phone, lifts the receiver, and holds it out to me. "Call the woman back and tell her no. Never mind. Anything."

"It's not any big deal," I say. "Really."

Hoot looks at me a long time, blinking. "Libby's not even in her grave yet, and here you are trying to fix me up with some woman I haven't even seen for fifty years. What are you doing here, butting in, interfering with my life, drinking my goddamn whiskey?"

"You got me wrong," I say, and I stand to go.

"Here, call her before you leave," he says, handing me the phone and the Dallas white pages. The phone number is already circled in light pencil inside, I've already noticed that. Hoot's is one of those old black hotel lobby phones with the metal dial and the old *Emerson* extension typed under the clear dial cover. Hoot paces back and forth across the kitchen, unable to bear looking at me, while I dial the number.

"Hello," I say to the woman's voice on the other end, but then the line goes dead. I look up and see Hoot holding down the receiver button with his thumb.

"All right," he says, "we'll give her a try. But I want you to make it a point to be here tomorrow evening before she is. You got me into this. If she doesn't fit the bill, *you're* the one who's telling her to go. I want somebody, *any*body, to take care of my Libby Fay, that's all, that's the only goddamn reason I'm going along with this, you follow?"

"Seemed like a good idea to me," I say, smiling again.

"Think you're pretty goddamn clever, don't you?" Hoot says. "Well, sir, you're not."

Next day, when I get back to Hoot's after one of my half-hearted job hunts, he's wearing a black clip-on bow tie and an ironed cotton shirt, and he's swimming in his own sweat.

"Don't we look spiffy?" I say.

"Oh, shut up," he says, "and quit being so goddamn cheerful, will you? Here, fix us some supper." He hands me a torn red-and-blue coupon and a check, already filled out in his shaky script, and I call in our usual order at Domino's, a three-topping large and three canned Cokes.

When the delivery boy rings the doorbell at 6 P.M., Hoot jumps in his chair at the breakfast table. We don't say anything to each other while we eat. Then the doorbell rings again at exactly seven, and Hoot drops a pizza slice into his lap. I don't say a word. I just wet a paper towel and try to wipe the tomato sauce off his shirt. Hoot says, "Leave me goddamn alone, will you? And go get that."

I open the door from the screened-in sleeping porch out to the front yard. "Arna Harkness?" I say.

She's a short, pear-shaped woman with dark skin and white-streaked black hair tied back into a braided ponytail between her shoulders. She's wearing a blue sweatshirt over orange Danskins, pink leg warmers, lime green Nikes.

"That's me," she says, smiling, but she looks to be a little disappointed that it's me who's answered the door.

I turn around to let her in and butt heads with Hoot, who's just walked up behind me. "Sorry," we both say, rubbing our foreheads and trying to get out of each other's way. Then Hoot holds his hand out to shake Arna Harkness's hand.

"Hello, Tom," Arna says.

"Long time," Hoot says.

"Yes. May I see Mrs. Ponder?"

"Yes," Hoot says, pumping her hand. "Thank you, yes. Please come on in."

"I don't understand why that bitch threw away all those pumpkins," Libby says to herself as we walk down the hallway to her bedroom. Hoot's decided to hang back in the kitchen all of a sudden, leaving me to explain everything to Arna Harkness.

When we both walk into her room, Libby stops mid-sentence and looks Arna up and down. Then she looks at me.

"Thomas," she says, her voice rattling and reedy, "I'm sorry, but this is between her and me. I think you should go now."

I look at Arna, and she nods for me to go. Then I walk into the hall, where Hoot's standing just outside the open door. He and I both lean together, listening.

"Mama," Libby says, "I've decided to marry that boy."

"He seems a little wild to me," Arna says.

"I know it, Mama," Libby says. "The language he uses, the way he swaggers. You and Papa are opposed, I know, but I've made up my mind."

"I understand," Arna says, sitting on the edge of Libby's bed. "The decision's yours, you know. Now, why don't we get you a bath, honey, get this hair of yours all washed and pretty?"

"Yes, Mama, thank you," Libby says. "It's been such a long time since you washed my hair."

Hoot and I look at each other, unable to believe what we're hearing, unable to believe our great good luck. Then we take turns ducking our heads into Libby's bedroom, watching Arna Harkness brush out Libby's matted hair.

In the kitchen thirty minutes later, Arna Harkness is washing dishes and I'm drying. She's got the sleeves of her sweatshirt rolled up, and she's already given Libby a sponge bath and changed her gown and bed linens. The washing machine is chugging away in the utility room.

"I don't like to talk money, Tom," Arna says, "so let's get that out of the way first thing." Hoot sits forward in his kitchen chair, quieter than I've ever seen him before in my life, his arms folded, his legs crossed, watching Arna Harkness at the sink. She gives a dirty plate a few quick swipes of the scouring pad in the suds of the left sink, then drops it into the right sink's scalding clear water. "My rate for a job like this one is usually ten dollars an hour. That's 7 A.M. to 7 P.M. weekdays, with an hour break at noon for lunch and another at two for 'The Young and the Restless,' plus nights and weekends off, unless there's an emergency, and then I *will* stay over, no overtime, no time and a half or double time, same pay, unless I'm asleep, and there's no charge for sleeping."

Arna sees me trying to use a pair of wooden spoons to fish out a stack of plates in the steaming water. She turns off the hot-water spigot, holds her hands under the cold water a moment, then plunges both hands into the scalding rinse water and holds the stack of plates out to me, smiling.

"I'll do most of what needs doing," she keeps on, "including some cleanup and cooking, and making up something for you to microwave from the freezer while I'm gone weekends." The last plate squeaks as she drops it into the rinse water. "There's a few other things you should know, too, Tom. I insist on doing things my way sometimes because sometimes my way is best and I know what I'm doing. I won't wait on anybody, not on any *able* body anyway, and I won't take any crap off a man. It's a promise I made myself a long time ago." She turns off the tap and looks back at Hoot, who's sitting so far forward in his kitchen chair he looks like he might fall off.

"You got any problems with all that?" she says.

Hoot looks at her a moment, then shakes his head.

"Do I have the job, then?"

Hoot nods his head and grins a little, he just can't help himself. "We'll give you a try," he says.

"All right, then, how about getting some paper and a pencil? And some more dish towels." Arna holds up her dripping hands like a surgeon after wash-up. "You got any more dry dish towels around here?"

Hoot opens two or three kitchen drawers before he finds a pencil and legal pad, then says, "Towels are in the hall closet. I'd go get you one myself, but—" He looks over at me to explain.

"He's got this thing about the hall closet," I tell her. "He won't go anywhere near it. That and the master bath. Here." I hand Arna my already-damp dish towel and say, "I'll go get us another one," then start for the hall.

But then Arna holds my arm, hands the wet towel back to me, and says, "Here, honey, let me go get it. I've got to find my way around this place anyway." She walks into the hall, opens the closet door, and says, "All right, gentlemen, which ones are the dish towels?"

"The blue ones with red stripes," Hoot says.

"Blue, red, green, purple," she says. "It's all the same to me, stripes, solids, or polka dots."

"I think she's color-blind," I tell Hoot.

"And proud of it," he whispers back. "Did you see that goddamn outfit she's wearing? Tacky."

"It's the stack of towels on the bottom shelf," I shout. "They're on the left, I think."

Arna walks back into the kitchen, tosses a dry dish towel to me over Hoot's head, and dries her hands with another. She looks at Hoot a moment, then says, "There's one other thing you should know, Tom," her voice grown hush all of a sudden. "This is the hard part, the part I never like, because I've been doing this kind of thing a long time, and I'm still not any good at doing this part. Sometimes, Tom, I get a feeling, you understand, and this is what the feeling tells me right now: You're not going to be needing my help around here for too long. You're going to need to be making some arrangements soon, you're going to need to be prepared." She folds the towel slowly, opens a drawer, and closes the drawer over the end of the towel, so that the towel hangs over.

"Do you understand what I'm saying here, Tom?"

Hoot looks at her, then at me, then out the kitchen window, and he nods.

"All right, then, sharpen your pencil. We got us a little shopping list to make. Then I've got to go." Arna sits across the table from Hoot, bends over to pull up her pink leg warmers, then sits up and rolls down her sleeves. "First thing tomorrow morning," she says, "you should go down to Sam's Wholesale Club and buy a case of those Depends undergarments and a box of Ace bandages. You'll also need to buy a good heating pad and a foam cushion for that bed in there, one of those pads that looks like an egg crate all rolled up. It should help heal the bedsores. Then you should get yourself a wok."

"I get plenty of walks," Hoot says, sitting up in his chair all of a sudden, sucking his gut in. "I'm in a lot better shape than I look."

"Wok," Arna says, then spells it out: "W-O-K. Go to the kitchen appliances department at Sam's and buy a hand-hammered wok from China, not one of those stainless steel electric jobs. They're too expensive, and they don't get the oil hot enough anyway."

"What does Libby need a goddamn wok for?" Hoot says, then catches himself. "Excuse my French."

"It's not just for your wife," Arna says. "Just get it. And get used to it. I'll buy everything else you need at the Kroger's on the way over here tomorrow morning. You *do* want me to start tomorrow morning, right?" Arna looks at the orange Swatch on her left wrist before Hoot can answer, then stands. "My God, I'm late for my Al-

Anon." Then, before we know it, she's run out of the house and started her car, an eighty-two yellow Subaru Brat parked out by the curb with a fist-sized rust hole in the muffler.

She reaches across the seat and rolls down the passenger window, revving her engine and shouting over the racket, "Gentlemen, get yourselves some rest tonight. Tomorrow, I'll be putting you both to work." Then Arna rolls her window back up, and we watch her peel rubber in her Brat, running through at least four gears by the time she gets down to the end of the block, her little truck backfiring three times just as she turns the corner.

"Well?" I ask Hoot.

"She's almost as loud as that outfit she's wearing and that goddamn car she's driving," Hoot says, "but she's pretty good with Libby. She's bossy as hell, too, but she'll do, I guess." Hoot turns away from me and heads back into the house, trying as hard as he can not to grin too hard, trying his best not to look too happy.

The next morning, when the doorbell rings at 7 A.M., I stagger, hung over and half asleep into the living room and open the front door. Arna's standing there in her white nurse's uniform and her lime green Nikes, holding a Kroger sack in each arm. "Get your shoes on and get the old man up," she says. "There's about twenty more bags of groceries in the truck."

When Hoot and I lay the last of the paper bags on the breakfast table, Arna hands Hoot a white cash register receipt so long that it drags on the kitchen floor. "I'll need a check for the full amount today," she says. "Otherwise, I'll be overdrawn at the bank."

Hoot looks at the receipt with his mouth open a little. Then we both watch Arna walk along the edge of the kitchen counter, opening all the cabinet doors top and bottom. "First thing we do around here," she says, "is we get rid of all the poison in this house." She reaches up and takes down the Morton's salt, holds it out so we can see the little girl with her umbrella on the label, and says, "hypertension"—then takes down the white sugar—"diabetes, hypoglycemia, hyperactivity"—and the white flour—"no nutrition, clogs the colon"—and she tosses everything into two paper sacks she's brought along just for the occasion.

Hoot moves in just ahead of her and takes a can of Folger's down from one of the shelves. "Got to get my motor started," he says, grinning, and starts scooping grinds into a filter for his Mr. Coffee machine. Before he can finish, though, Arna's already swiped the coffee can out of his hand and tossed it, too.

"Not my coffee," Hoot says. "Goddamn, you can't throw out my coffee."

"You put me in charge now, remember? I got you decaf."

Arna moves to the cabinet next to the fridge, looks at the rows of Campbell's cream of chicken soup, and shakes her head. "Is this the only food you've got in this house, Tom? Is this what you've been feeding your wife for the last three months?"

"It's the only thing she'll eat anymore," Hoots says. "It's the only thing I can cook."

"Nonsense," she says, dropping the soup cans into a sack. "And what about you and Travis? Is this all you've been feeding yourselves around here, too?"

Hoot looks at me and says nothing.

"Pizzas," I say. "Lately, we've been eating pizzas."

"My God, Tom," Arna says, "how do you expect to take care of your wife if you refuse to take care of yourself?"

Arna opens the refrigerator door, takes down the sticks of butter from their tray, and tosses them into a sack, then the bacon and the half-and-half and the cheddar cheese. She opens the cap to the carton of whole milk, takes a sniff, and holds her nose, then pours it all down the drain.

"There," she says, leaning back against the counter. "Tom, you and Travis take these canned goods and staples to the Salvation Army on your way over to Sam's. We'll throw the rest out. I hate to waste food, but these perishables must've perished at least three months ago anyway.

"Now, for the good stuff, " Arna says, reaching into a bag on the breakfast table, rattling the paper while she pulls out a box of oatmeal, a bunch of bananas, and a plastic bag filled with something that looks like potting soil. "Gentlemen, I give you breakfast. Rolled oats, wheat germ, and bananas."

Just as we're about to finish putting all the groceries away, Arna opens the cabinet over the fridge, the only one she hasn't opened yet, and she lets out a little scream.

Hoot and I look at each other.

Arna stands there in front of the fridge, her hands on her hips, looking at row upon row of Jim Beam in half-gallon bottles.

"Tom," she says, turning to Hoot, "we've got us a problem here."

"Heartbreak," Hoot says and raises his glass of apple juice.

I can't hear him say it because I'm sweeping the patio out back and he's saying it from the other side of the kitchen window. I know what he's saying, though, and I know what he's drinking. He takes a sip, makes a pained face, and gives me that pitiful look of his, then gets back to work.

After two hours of argument this morning—Arna refusing the whole time to work in a house that she said was "plumbed with whiskey"—Hoot finally promised her that he'd keep the Jim Beam in the garage with all the other flammables and that he wouldn't drink a drop of the hard stuff while she was here. Since settling that argument, Arna's kept us both busy most of the day, Hoot and I making six trips to six different stores between the two of us, then mowing the yard, edging the sidewalk, and clipping the hedges. She got me started sweeping the porch an hour ago. Now she's got Hoot slicing peppers and bok choy and water chestnuts for stir-fry in the kitchen.

"Travis," Arna shouts, leaning out the back door, "you'd better finish here and get cleaned up now. I need you to set the table."

In the kitchen thirty minutes later, she passes me a bowl of hot and sour soup, a plate of fried brown rice, and her specialty, walnut chicken, Szechwan style. "I made up a special batch without the red chilies for Libby," Arna says. "She just loved the soup, Tom. It put her right to sleep. And she's sleeping a whole lot better now with that foam mattress pad you bought her."

Hoot grunts something and sips loudly from his soup spoon, then picks out something from his soup he can't recognize and holds it up. "What's this?"

"A tiger lily stem," Arna says. She watches Hoot pick out a few of the stems in his soup, laying them on his napkin one by one, then folding his arms and moping a while. "You're still upset about our argument this morning, aren't you, Tom?" she says. "You shouldn't be, you know. You made the right decision. It's the best thing for Libby. It's the best thing for you."

"A goddamn teetotaler, wouldn't you know it," Hoot says under his breath, looking over at me and rolling his eyes. Then he looks at Arna. "Since when did you start calling my wife *Libby*? That's what I'd like to know. You got awfully chummy with my wife all of a sudden. Hell, she won't even *talk* to me, takes one look at me—her husband!—and she screams."

"Try not to take it personally," Arna says. "She's not herself, Tom, you know that."

"That's easy for you to say," Hoot says. "I don't think I can take it anymore." He spoons out a rubbery black thing and holds it up. "All right, what the hell is this?"

"It's just a tree fungus," Arna says, then turns to me. "So, Travis, have you got yourself a girl?"

Hoot perks up now, grins at me, lifts up his cup of hot tea.

"I was married a while," I say, "but then I got divorced." I reach across the table for the soy sauce.

"I'm sorry to hear that," Arna says, then waits, I suppose, for me to explain. I look over at Hoot.

"That's about all you're going to get out of this boy. He's not much of a talker."

"I've got a grandniece and a grandnephew about your age, Travis, who both just got divorced," Arna starts in. "Gerald—he's the son of Angela, my daughter by my first husband, who was a drunkard— Gerald's just gone crazy with the married women. It's not enough that he shot his own marriage down. He's determined to take a few others down with him. Terri—she's the daughter of Morris, my son by my second husband, who, God forgive me, was another drunk- ard—Terri, she's another story altogether. Two months to the day after her wedding, she left her husband a note on the kitchen table with the phone number of a prostitute and a maid service, saying those were all he needed anyway, and she moved out. She's a sweet girl really—pretty, too, which can be more of a curse than a blessing sometimes—but she learns fast." Arna scoops up some rice and veg- gies with her fork and takes a bite. "You know, Travis," she says,

"maybe I should get Terri to come over here sometime and visit us."
She winks at me and smiles with her mouth full, a grain of rice stuck
to the tip of her nose.

"I don't know," I say.

Just then, I hear Libby calling from her bedroom, and I'm more
than a little grateful for the interruption.

"I'll go check on her," Arna says, pushing her kitchen chair out
and standing up, then looking at Hoot. "Tell you what, Tom, why
don't you come with me?"

"No, ma'am. I don't like scaring my own wife half to death. It's
too goddamn much for the both of us."

"Come on," Arna says, taking Hoot by the arm and helping him
to his feet. "Just come along and see what happens."

Hoot shrugs his shoulders and looks at me. "Travis, why don't you
join us?" he says. "Just like a goddamn Halloween party."

I stand up and push my chair out, then follow Hoot and Arna
Harkness down the hall to Libby's bedroom.

"The piano tuner hasn't got any clothes on, and he lives on a
luxury liner," Libby says as Arna opens the bedroom door. She
laughs in her bed, then looks at her splinted fingers, at her sparrow-
boned hand still wrapped in a fiberglass cast. She looks up at Arna
and me, and when she sees Hoot, she doesn't scream.

"I'm so glad that we could all be here together," Libby says, then
stares at Hoot a long time.

"Papa," she tells Hoot, "Thomas and I have something very important to tell you. Despite your unreasonable objections these last
few weeks, we've both decided to marry. Please understand, we're not
asking for your permission, but Mama has given us her blessing, and
we would like your blessing as well."

"God," Hoot says. "Goddamn." Then he leaves the room.

In the kitchen a few minutes later, he's pacing around the breakfast
table. "Who's that woman in there? She's killing me."

"She's just going back, Tom," Arna says. "It happens that way all
the time. It really doesn't have that much to do with you."

"Her father," Hoot says, "of all the goddamn people. Hell, I was better off when she thought I was a communist. Her old man was a son of a bitch who didn't deserve her. He cut her off, wouldn't talk to her, wouldn't have a thing to do with her, all because she married another son of a bitch who didn't deserve her."

"Why don't you just go back in there and play along?" Arna says. "It can't hurt anything, and it just might do some good."

"Why should I do something for that son of a bitch? He never did a goddamn thing for us. He never did anything for Libby but give her a lot of grief."

"You wouldn't be doing it for him," Arna says.

Back in Libby's room a few minutes later, Hoot sits on the edge of her bed, takes her good hand, and says, "Libby Fay, I give you my blessing."

"Thank you, Papa," Libby says, then puts her arms around Hoot's neck, closes her eyes, and kisses him on the mouth.

When she opens her eyes again, she looks at Hoot a moment, blinks, then kisses him on the mouth again, this time a long kiss that makes Arna and me both look away. "Thomas," Libby says, breathless, "where did you run off to? I've just bought some new sheet music, and I wanted you to hear me play it."

Arna looks at me, and we both step into the hallway. Then she closes the door quietly behind us to leave Hoot and Libby together alone.

———————

"Heartbreak," I say two weeks later and lift my glass of Jim Beam, but Hoot's in no mood for horseplay and I'm in no mood for drinking. Just the smell of the straight whiskey Hoot's poured for me has made me dizzy and a little sick at my stomach, so I put the glass back down on the breakfast table and watch Hoot stare out the kitchen window.

My Aunt Libby is dead, Arna Harkness is gone, and I'm trying to find the heart to tell Hoot I'm moving out.

He's still wearing the same cotton shirt and slacks he wore to the funeral three days ago, except the shirt isn't white anymore, the yellow circles under his arms are turning brown, and his body odor and the sour whiskey smell on his breath are harder to take than they were when I sat next to him in the church pew while the organist played Libby's last Debussy, "The Girl with the Flaxen Hair."

The morning Arna woke Hoot to tell him that Libby had died in the night, he stood from his bed in the guest bedroom next to mine, walked past Libby's room without stopping to look inside, and went straight to the garage.

Arna saw him standing at the kitchen door with a half gallon of Jim Beam under each arm and said, "Tom, take care of yourself."

"She was my wife," he said. "Leave me goddamn alone, will you?"

Hoot sat down at the breakfast table and broke the seals of both bottles. Arna called the ambulance and the funeral home from the phone in Libby's room, then left a note for Hoot to mail her her last check. After that, she left. I called her at her apartment a few hours later to ask her why.

"I don't see much point in either one of us enabling the man or taking his abuse," she said. "It just makes things a lot worse."

"He'll drink himself to death," I said.

"I doubt it. And if he does, that's his problem. It's all pretty predictable, really. I might've been surprised if he'd just dealt with it straight on and not taken the easy way out. There's a man for you."

"Are you going to the funeral?" I asked.

"I'm not much on funerals, honey, no," Arna said. "We've done about as much as we can do there, Travis. You need to get out of that house, get yourself a job, get your mind off that girl. Tom's got to find his own way on this one. So do you. You've put off facing this thing long enough."

Still staring out the kitchen window, Hoot sits up in his chair. "It was always in the back of my mind that she was damn near old enough to be my mother," he says, "but I guess I always took it for granted she'd outlive me. I guess I'm a stupid son of a bitch."

He doesn't say anything after that. The sun's going down inside the leaves of the cottonwood in Hoot's backyard, and it's starting to get dark and too quiet, so I decide to tell him.

"Got a job today."

He nods his head.

"It's with a business machine company. Selling copiers mostly. The money's good, but I'll be on the road three or four months at a time."

Hoot looks at me. "You know, I've always wondered why the hell you keep hanging around this place. What the hell are you doing here?"

"I don't know," I say.

"Then get the hell out," Hoot says and looks back out the kitchen window. "Get out," he says again.

As I'm throwing the last of my gear into the backseat of my Volare in the front drive, Hoot appears with his drink in his hand at the screened door of his sleeping porch.

I start my car. I look at Hoot on the porch. "Thank you, sir," he says and raises his glass.

———

Eight months later, I'm just starting to unload my suitcases on the daybed in my East Dallas efficiency when I get a call from my father. I've been on the outs with the man for years, so I'm a little surprised to hear from him. When I hear his voice, I get this sinking feeling.

"What's wrong, Dad?" I say.

"Did you hear about Hoot?" he says.

"No," I say. I'm expecting the worst, I admit it.

"The old bastard got hitched. About three weeks ago. Can you believe that? You missed the party, Travis. It was one hell of a party."

Right away, I lie to my father to get him off the phone, tell him my bathtub is overflowing and leaking into my landlady's apartment downstairs. Then I hang up fast and call Hoot's house first thing. Arna answers the phone.

"Travis, honey," she says, "you were the very first person we called to invite to our backyard luau when we got back from Maui."

"I've been out of town," I say. "Sorry I missed it."

"You're not going to miss a thing," she says. "Why don't you just come on over tonight, and we'll just have us another little luau in your honor? We'd love to see you."

"I don't know," I say.

When I drive my Volare up Hoot's driveway, the grass on the center hump is freshly mowed like the cross-cut golf grass in the front yard. Except for that and the English ivy, trimmed to the edges of Hoot's sleeping porch out front, everything still looks pretty much the same. Then I see the Japanese lanterns hanging from the eaves of the house and hear the music coming through the open windows, ukuleles and steel guitars and Don Ho singing:

> I want to go back to my little grass shack
> in Kealakekua Hawai'i
> where the humuhumunukunukapua'a
> go swimming by.

I ring the doorbell next to the sleeping porch's screened door, and they both appear on the porch, Arna wearing a muumuu with a blinding floral pattern of splashed tropical colors, Hoot wearing a matching aloha shirt and a straw hat, holding out a glass of Hawaiian Punch in one hand and what looks like a crushed bouquet of flowers in the other.

"Goddamn, Travis," Hoot says, "you look like hell."

"Thanks a lot," I say. "It's good to see you, too."

"You need to lighten up, boy, have yourself some fun." Hoot hands me the Hawaiian Punch, and I sip carefully from the straw, trying to keep from poking my eye out with the point of the paper parasol in the hurricane glass. "I'd fix you a Mai-Tai," Hoot says, "but I'm a teetotaler now." He grins at Arna. "Honey, this boy's too serious. We need to get this boy *lei*-ed."

"That's tacky, Tom," Arna says and slaps him on the wrist.

"Don't you be telling me about tacky," he says, then puts his arm around her waist. "Honey, I didn't know what tacky was till you came into my life."

"He's a poet," Arna says.

"And she's my Indian princess," Hoot says.

They both kiss each other with a loud smack, and Hoot rolls his eyes at me. "Enough to make you want to throw up, isn't it, Travis?" He gives Arna the lei he's been crushing in his hand, and I duck down so she can put it around my neck. "What the hell are we all standing around out here for?" Hoot says. "Travis, come on inside."

"This is all a little hard to get used to," I say after I sit on the couch, looking around the living room at the bright vases of dried flowers, the bowls of conches and seashells, the coconuts and wrinkled sea horses and inflated blowfishes all netted in one corner of the living room. Only Libby's white baby grand is the same, angled into the opposite corner, clean, dusted, uncluttered.

Hoot limps to the armchair across from me, and Arna sits backward on the piano stool next to him.

"So," I ask, "how's everything been going?"

"The truth is, Travis," Hoot says, "I got tallywacker troubles. My tallywacker's all out of wack. I've been prostrated to my prostate."

"Enough already," Arna says, slapping Hoot on the knee. "Travis, this man here had to go to four different urologists before they finally got his diagnosis right."

"Doctors," Hoot says, "sons of bitches."

"They ran all kinds of tests on him and gave him all kinds of pills," Arna says. "It wasn't until he got this new doctor that he started making any progress at all. The doctor got him off all the pills and put him on a restrictive diet and prescribed sex once a day as the main treatment. Seems to be working out just fine." Arna looks over at Hoot and smiles.

"It's just about to kill me," he says, blushing. "That and my god-damn bursitis."

"When he first proposed to me three months ago, Travis," Arna starts in, "I told him, 'No, Tom, I'm sorry, but I just can't marry you. I've been taking care of people all my life. It's not that I'm tired of doing it or even that I mind so much. I just don't have any desire to marry somebody who's either sick or drunk or crazy, just to be their nurse. I've nursed one drunk father, two drunk husbands, and God knows how many sick patients and crying babies, and that's enough for me, thank you, I'd rather nurse myself awhile.' Travis, I'm telling you, this man had been showing up to my Al-Anon meetings for months, bugging me to death and swearing he'd never drink another drop of whiskey again if I'd just marry him. Well, I just didn't trust it, you understand. Then one night he showed up at a meeting with a poem and single-stem rose and a bunch of bluebonnets he'd picked himself out in Waxahachie. He got down on one knee and read his poem aloud, then volunteered to start the meeting by reading the twelve steps. I just couldn't resist him any longer after that."

"That's sweet," I say.

"Oh, shut up," Hoot says, "and let her tell it."

"Well," Arna says, "you can see how it all turned out. I've been nursing the poor man ever since we got back from Maui. His little limp is just pitiful, don't you think?"

"It's your own goddamn fault," Hoot says. "You were the one that came up with the bubble bath idea." Hoot looks over at me. "I'm pretty sure I strained it in the bathtub."

"Strained what?" I say.

"My tallywacker," Hoot says. "What else?"

"I can think of a few other things that might've strained it," Arna says, winking at me.

"Do you have to talk about it like that?" Hoot asks her, then looks back at me, blushing again. "I'm telling you, Travis, the woman's got no modesty whatsoever."

"This man hadn't taken a bath in a year, Travis," Arna butts in. "That was the problem. For months, he'd been stripping down to his birthday suit in the kitchen early mornings and giving himself a sponge bath in the kitchen sink. You didn't know about that, did you, Travis?"

"I guess I didn't notice," I say. I'm lying, of course.

"I finally got it out of him one morning after I'd slipped in his puddle on the kitchen floor and almost broke my neck," Arna says. "It wasn't safe, I told him. It wasn't hygienic, I said, eating and bathing in the same room. I said, 'Tom, honey, I love you, but you've got BO, do you know that?' I said, 'Honey, what in God's name have you got against taking a bath?'

"Then he said, 'It's where she fell.'

"Well, Travis," Arna says, "right then, it was all perfectly clear to me what I had to do. I just walked out and got into my Brat, drove down to the Sam's Wholesale Club and bought a king-size box of Mr. Bubble.

"When the bathroom was full of steam and the tub was full and foamy with bubbles, I dragged Tom into the bathroom and told him to strip naked. I said, 'Tom, you're worse than my son Morris when he was five years old.' I said, 'Get in that tub, Tom, and don't get out till I tell you to.'

"About thirty minutes later, Travis, I heard him yell, 'Can I get out now?' I was in the kitchen stir-frying some Moo Goo Gai Pan. I said, 'Have you soaked off all the stink yet?' and he said, 'Yes, ma'am,' and I said, 'Well, I guess you can get out, then.'

"I didn't hear anything from him for a while, Travis. Then after about five minutes he yelled, 'Help! I can't get out.'"

"She'd put in too much goddamn Mr. Bubble," Hoot puts in. "I was slick as a duck in an oil spill. I was sliding all over, cracking my skull on the ceramic soap dish, going under the water, breathing in suds by the lungful. I was drowning trying to get out of the goddamn bathtub."

"Well, Travis," Arna goes on, "I tried to help him out. He was still weak from being seasick the whole trip back from Maui on the Royal Viking. By the time I got to the bathroom, he'd already worn himself out, too, and he was in a panic. On top of everything else, he was heavy, and I couldn't get a good grip on his hand or any other part of him, and he'd sloshed all around and splashed suds all over the bathroom floor, so I was having enough trouble trying to stand on my own two feet, much less trying to get him out of that tub.

"After a while, I said, 'Tom, I'm getting in there with you,' and he said, 'What the hell for? You trying to drown us both?' and I said, 'I can't pull you out, so I'm going to try pushing you.'

"Well, Travis, I took off all my clothes, and I climbed in there with Tom, and right away I smelled the Moo Goo Gai Pan burning and I remembered I'd forgotten to turn the gas down. About that time I realized I wasn't going to get myself out of the tub either, much less get Tom out, and right away I knew I'd made a big mistake getting in there in the first place."

"Just about then," Hoot says, "it hit me." He starts to say something, but it catches in his throat and he looks over at Arna.

"That's about the time Tom remembered about Libby falling," Arna says. "Up till then, he'd been blocking it out, you understand, and then it all just came back to him in a rush. The two of us sat there in that tub, naked as the day we were born, and he just held on to me and remembered it all and told me all about it, told me how he'd tried to lift Libby out of the bathtub after she'd fallen. She was too heavy, he told me, and he was too afraid he might hurt her any more than she already was, so he held her head above the water till the tub drained. Then he had to leave her there for the longest time to call the ambulance, had to wait even longer for the ambulance to come, had to cover her when he heard the sirens outside because she was unconscious and he knew she wouldn't want anybody to see her like that. Then he told me how it took three strapping paramedics the longest time to get her out of that tub and onto that stretcher. We both sat there in that tub for the longest time, Travis, and he held on to me and told me all about it. The Moo Goo Gai Pan was burning in the kitchen, and the house was going to burn down around us, was going to boil us both alive in a tub of Mr. Bubble, but I just had to hold on to him a little while longer, you understand, he just had to grieve a little bit more.

"Well, Travis," Arna says, "when that was over, Tom let go of me and knocked himself on the head and said, 'I'm a stupid son of a bitch.' Then he pulled the chain for the tub's drain plug. We both sat there until the water was all sucked out, and we rinsed the soap off ourselves and rinsed out the tub, and we got out all right. Half the house was filled with smoke, the Moo Goo Gai Pan was burnt beyond fixing, and our shins and elbows were black and blue, but it looked like we were going to get to live together in this world a little bit longer."

Arna looks at Hoot, and he sits forward in his armchair. "To make a long goddamn story short, Travis," he says, "that's the first and last goddamn time I take a goddamn bubble bath." Then he sits back in his chair again and takes a sip of his Hawaiian Punch.

"So," I say, "how was your trip to Maui?"

"Libby made the reservations at the Sheraton Kaanapali a long time back," Arna says, "but Tom had forgotten all about it. I asked him if staying there would bother him and he said no, he thought Libby wouldn't've minded at all, not under the circumstances, so we stayed there in one of the bridal suites. I bought this at the *wikiwiki* market right across the street." Arna picks up a black doll from the fireplace mantel and hands it to me. It's a hula girl with a grass skirt and round breasts and both arms swaying together, all carved out of black pumice. "We ate *mahimahi* at the Hotel luau," Arna says. "We danced till six in the morning, and everybody there thought I was a local."

"The woman just about killed me," Hoot says. "I don't think I'll ever get over it."

"I'm making *mahimahi* tonight, Travis," Arna says, "that and a salad with papaya seed dressing. The *mahimahi*'s really canned white tuna, but I won't tell our other guest if you don't."

I hand Arna her black hula doll back, watch her put it back on the fireplace mantel, watch it do its frozen swaying dance between Libby's two white ceramic ballerinas.

"What other guest?" I start to say.

But then, just then, wouldn't you know it, the doorbell rings.

Arna walks to the door, puts her hand on the doorknob and turns to me.

"I hope you don't mind," she says. "I meant to tell you earlier."

When Arna opens the door, in walks a black-haired girl in her early thirties. Her hair is braided into a long ponytail that falls down between her shoulder blades to her waist.

Hoot and I both stand at the same time, holding our glasses of Hawaiian Punch.

"Travis," Arna says, "Terri, my grandniece."

"Terri," Hoot says, "Travis, my grandnephew."

I can't make up my mind whether to shake her hand or not, so I don't. Then Hoot hands me another lei he's been crushing in his hand all night. When I see Hoot's eyes, I see the girl through them. I watch fifty years pass over his face, see the same face he must have worn when he first saw his light-haired Libby Fay at the Lone Star Gas Company in 1933, the same face he must have worn when he first saw his dark-haired Arna Harkness at the Texas State Tuberculosis Sanatorium in 1934. I see this look on Hoot's face, and my hands tremble just the slightest bit as I put the lei around her neck.

Hoot looks over at me. He grins and raises his glass of Hawaiian Punch.

"Heartbreak," he says.

Influenza

I was sick with the flu—I knew it—but I wanted to kiss my wife. My forehead and my neck were hot, my throat was sore, my lungs and my shoulders ached, and for the first time in a while I was in the mood.

When I leaned over Nina's drafting table in her study down the hall from our bedroom, I planted one on her mouth, but she kept scribbling on her plans for remodeling La Esperanza, a local San Antonio strip mall. She'd been moonlighting on the project for months, staying up till two or three in the morning week after week, just to meet her deadline for preliminary drawings.

I kissed her again.

"What are you doing?" she said.

She glanced at me a moment, then went back to work on the elevations she'd sketched. She rolled out a new sheet of tracing paper, smoothed it out onto the sketches overlaying each other, then with her soft-lead pencil refined the details of the glass storefront, the stucco panels, the oak-veneer beams. The desk lamp over her head lit the fine hairs that grew along her jaw and lengthened into the dark *V* at the back of her neck. When I touched her throat, she dropped her pencil.

"Don't you have work to do?"

In my study across the hall, I sat at my desk, opened my briefcase, and took out the report I had to have translated in two weeks for the bank's branch office in Mexico City.

The first word I'd written was *The*. I looked at this word a while but couldn't get past it. "*The*," I thought. "What does this word mean?"

I scratched through the word and wrote *Nina*.

The next word, *influence*, I scratched through and changed as well. Then the next. And the next.

In an hour, the report was finished. I felt terrible and wonderful.

Next morning, the digital thermometer read 102 degrees, so I called in sick at the bank and stayed in bed. I pulled the comforter up to my chin. I squinted my eyes shut and pretended to sleep while I watched Nina dress.

It was like nothing I'd ever seen before, the fever was so clarifying. The way she stepped into her muslin skirt, the way her silk blouse fell into folds over her hips, it was all I could do to keep quiet.

She sat next to me on our bed with her briefcase at her feet. I was shivering by then.

"Raymond," she whispered, "before I leave for the office, can I get you anything? Tylenol? Seven-Up?"

I folded back the blankets on her side of the bed. It was difficult for me to talk. I tried but couldn't swallow. I held her cool hands.

"Stay with me today, Nina. Come to bed. Call them up and tell them all to go to hell."

"I'll call Dr. Spiegal," she said, "right away."

That day, while Nina was gone, the thermometer's readout rose to 104 degrees, but I couldn't stay in bed. It was February, but I spent hours in the garage sitting naked on the concrete floor. I ripped open twenty or thirty cardboard boxes before I found the Polaroids I'd taken of her on Padre Island beaches the summer we met at the University of Texas. I called her office ten, fifteen times.

"I'm in a meeting," she said. "Can't this wait?"

When she got home from work that night, she laid a Target sack at the foot of our bed, turned her back to me, and unbuttoned her blouse. She reached behind and unhooked her bra, and the muscles at the small of her back rippled and tensed; her scapulae flared just so, like wings.

She opened a dresser drawer, unfolded an old UT sweatshirt, and slipped it over her head, her arms high in the air. For the first time in my life I saw the faint and intricate blue veining of her breasts, and I started to cough. I coughed until tears came into my eyes. I coughed and I wept.

Nina sat on the edge of our bed and put her palm to my forehead.

"There there," she said.

With my forefinger I traced along her sweatshirt's collar, across from her collarbone to her throat, then down.

"Stop," she said and held my wrist.

"You're cruel," I told her.

"No," she said, "you're sick."

She reached into the sack at the foot of our bed and lined the nightstand with bottles of Bayer and Nyquil and vitamin C. She pulled a vaporizer from the bottom of the sack, and in a while steam plumed out over the bed till the sheets were soft with moisture and heat. When she returned from the kitchen, she carried a bowl of tomato soup and a pitcher of spring water on a tray.

She filled my water glass, dropping each pill into my palm and tipping the glass to my mouth each time I swallowed. She fed me spoonfuls of hot soup.

"Lots of liquids," she said, "and plenty of rest," but nothing she could have said at that moment would have consoled me.

The next day I felt better, but when I flipped through the ruined report in my study, I said, "What have I done?"

I dressed in a rush in our bedroom.

"Where are you going?" Nina said.

"To work. Otherwise, I'll never get caught up."

Nina didn't get dressed. She lay in our bed, her head propped up with her pillow, her face flushed, her hands holding the comforter to her chin as if she were a cat peering over a curb.

"You did this to me, Raymond," she said. "You kissed me and you knew."

"I don't know what you're talking about," I said.

"It's all right, Raymond. You can kiss me again."

I bent to kiss her forehead, but she tilted her head back, her eyes closed, her mouth open as if to receive communion.

"Here." I handed her the glass of orange juice I'd poured myself in the kitchen, and she stared at the glass as I hurried around the room, refilling the vaporizer and turning it on, lining up all the bottles on the nightstand in a row.

"If you need anything else," I said, "you can call me at the office."

"There is one other thing, before you go." She nodded toward the bathroom. "The Mentholatum. In the medicine cabinet." She smiled.

In the bathroom I threw open the cabinet door and fumbled for the jar, dropping Nina's empty cold cream jars and medicine bottles into the wastebasket until I found it. When I came back to our room, Nina had opened her nightgown.

"Stay home, Raymond." Her voice was hoarse and deep. "Rub my chest."

I handed her the Mentholatum, then left. I wanted nothing to do with her.

That morning she called the bank every hour on the hour, that afternoon every thirty minutes. I couldn't work.

That night I stayed late at Mi Tierra's, eating cabrito and drinking Tres Equis. It was after midnight when I came home. All the lights in the house were out, but I could hear the shower running. I opened the hall closet and unfolded a blanket. I lay on the couch and turned off the lamp. I tried to sleep.

"Raymond?"

Nina sat on the coffee table in the dark, her wet hair curled into loops over her eyes, droplets falling onto her breasts, pooling into her navel, onto the table around her.

"Where are your clothes?" I touched her leg. It was hot. I covered her with my blanket, then carried her to bed. I sat by her and gave her sips of spring water. "Do you feel any better?"

She shivered under the comforter and shook her head. "I feel terrible. I feel—" She smiled.

"Why are you looking at me like that?" I said.

Then she kissed me.

"Please don't," I said.

She kissed me again. It was a wet kiss, the kiss of a girl who would be drunk for the first time, sitting alone on a long gray beach, trying to remove the beach tar from the heels of her bare feet.

"Stop it," I said. Then I tasted the sea.

My fever returned.

For six days we lay sick together. We never dressed, never left our bed, except to move to the balcony, to the wet bar, to her drafting table. We ate nothing, said nothing; we sweated till we ached; we never answered the phone, never slept. The floors of the house were covered with wadded balls of white paper, with scattered clothes, with torn sketches and blueprints. Everything went to hell, and I was never so happy.

When I woke at 5 A.M. the last morning, I reached across the bed in the dark for her; I reached until I touched the edge of the bed.

She was in her study, already dressed for work, folding up the ironing board, putting away the iron, the digital thermometer between her teeth.

"Ninety-eight point six," she said, then held the thermometer out to me as if I wouldn't believe her. The pockets and sleeves of her blouse were stiff, the pleats of her skirt all sharp creases, straight, symmetrical. Only a little steam was left in the room.

"This has been the worst week of my life, Raymond," she said. "I don't think I'll ever catch up."

"What?" I said.

At 1 A.M. the next morning, she was still drawing at her drafting table. She lowered her T-square across the tracing paper, drew a line, moved her triangle across the top of the T-square, drew another.

"Are you coming to bed?" I asked her.

She looked up from her working drawings—all straight lines, perpendicular and horizontal, rows and rows of stanchions and roof tiles and bricks.

"I'm staying in here tonight." She nodded to the daybed the Sears truck had delivered that afternoon. "I don't want to bother you." She looked down at the long white sheet of tracing paper taped to her drawing table and began drawing again.

A moment later, I heard her say, "How do you feel?"

I had already left her study by then. I was half the way to our bedroom, running my hand along the long hallway wall for the light switch in the dark.

"I feel better," I said. "Any time now, I think I'll be over this."

Godzilla
vs.
the
Sensitive
Man

Eight months after his wife, Trixie, left with the Episcopal priest, their marriage counselor at St. James, Dr. Marshall Corley began to have inappropriate and unsettling thoughts about Rose Kindred, one of his new patients.

He'd never had such a problem before. If he entered an examination room and an attractive woman was lying face down on the adjustment table, he had no reason to think about it. As a chiropractic care physician, he didn't often find it necessary to ask his patients to disrobe, except for the initial screening to test the straightness of the spine, and when he did most spinal manipulations, his patients were fully dressed. The clinic's X-ray technician, sports medicine expert, and masseuse Jean, his new partner, was far more likely to see patients unclothed, and he was glad of it. Or, to be more accurate, before Rose Kindred, he was simply indifferent. He was human, of course—that's the way he put it to himself—and if, on occasion, he found his thoughts straying during an adjustment, he would immediately begin talking about the forecast for sleet, or the Cubs, or his new hobby, collecting videotapes and memorabilia of the science fiction horror movies and TV series he'd loved as a kid. Before Rose, there'd never been any problem.

Besides, at first, Dr. Corley wouldn't have called Rose attractive, at least not in any noticeable way, when she came in to the clinic for her first visit. If anything, he found her coarse, almost repulsive, because of the language she used. And he was distracted, rushed, trying to get settled into the new clinic he'd decided to build right after Trixie left him for the priest—he couldn't bring himself to use the man's name, the man he'd trusted to help him try to rebuild his marriage of five years after the birth of a stillborn child.

Rose's charts showed that she'd first come to the clinic barely able to straighten out or walk, reporting a common complaint—severe muscle spasms in her lower back that had caused her to miss work the week before as a cashier at the Murphysboro Wal-Mart. She'd been having chronic back pain for months but, after helping a co-worker in Stationery stock the shelves and picking up a large box of envelopes with her back instead of her legs, she'd had to spend two days in bed, on muscle relaxants and painkillers.

Dr. Corley's receptionist, Kari, showed Rose into the X-ray consultation room and turned on the new VCR machine to show a videotape he'd recently made that explained common spinal misalignments—subluxations—to save the trouble of having to repeat himself too often in the education phase of his consultations. With his new clinic, and the many new clients drawn to the new building and "the state-of-the-art diagnostic and sports medicine facilities," as he called them in his new pamphlet, he didn't have time to waste on unnecessary or repetitive minor details. To pay all the bills for his new clinic, he had to move patients along as quickly as possible, without, if possible, losing that human touch.

When he came into the consultation room, Rose had been sitting there for fifteen minutes after the videotape should have come to an end, much longer than he would have liked, but he'd been running behind, telling the painting subcontractor what a botched job he'd done trying to rush putting up the wallpaper in the women's room. Rose sat there in an ergonomic chair, running her index finger down the plastic spinal skeleton mounted to the consultation table.

"My best girlfriend for twenty years runs off with my old man— the bitch and the son of a bitch, I call them—and then my goddamn back goes out. What you think, Doc? You think there's any connection?"

It was the first thing Rose ever said to him, and she laughed when she said it.

At first, Dr. Corley didn't know how to respond to such a statement, to such questions, to her laughter. Then he said what he'd told many patients: "Studies *do* suggest a connection between psychological and physiological pain." She gave him a frown that made him realize how formal he sounded—a reaction, he supposed, to her coarse language—so he tried to be less formal.

"Something terrible happens to us that throws us off balance emotionally, and we can lose our balance in other ways. The kind of back pain you feel now most likely has to do with your body's being out of balance, and maybe that has something to do with the pain you feel about your husband and your friend." Still too formal, he thought, but he'd said what he'd meant. He was being direct, tactful. Sensitive.

Then, just at that moment, he glanced down at Rose's blue Wal-Mart smock shirt, saw how large her breasts were, how well shaped, and in a rush of fear returned his eyes to hers. She hadn't seen his glance, but his face flushed with warmth, and he remembered something his sister, who was large-breasted, had said about a mechanic who had stared at her breasts the entire time he explained what was wrong with her Toyota's air-conditioning compressor. "Listen, buster," she'd told the mechanic, as she related the story at a family get-together in Marion, "I'd appreciate it if you'd talk to *me* and not to my tits." Dr. Corley had never considered his sister, or her stories, particularly funny, and remembering this story now made his face flush even more, made him feel off balance himself.

He continued, explaining the standard diagnostic procedures and possible therapy strategies, including manipulation and physical therapy. Because he was running behind, he told Rose he'd have Jean begin electro-stimulation massage therapy on her lower back today, to help reduce her muscle spasms and chronic pain. He told her to buy an ice pack and lay it at the small of her back that night to help reduce inflammation. Then he asked Rose to schedule two appointments with Kari—one with Jean to have diagnostic X-rays made tomorrow, then another with him so he could give Rose a full examination the day after.

For some reason, the words *a full examination* stuck in his mind, unsettled him. He stood from his chair in the consultation room and said, "Any questions?"

Rose flexed the spinal vertebrae back and forth on the consultation table.

"Look, Doc, I'm going to be real honest with you, okay? I didn't watch your little movie, and I've got a problem with all this stuff you've been throwing at me. My mama thinks I'm nuts going to a back-cracker, but I'm desperate, all right? I just don't think I can keep standing on my feet on the goddamn concrete floor checking people's stuff out all day with this pain. They say my insurance'll pay for most of it, so I'll try you out. Tell you what, I'll give you a month. If I'm still hurting a month from now, then I'm probably going to call it quits with you people. How's that?"

At first, he had no idea how to respond. Then he smiled and said, "It's not uncommon for me to encounter skepticism and resistance to chiropractic care, but if you give me and my staff a chance to work with you, I think you'll be pleased with not only the management of your pain but also your overall health care."

He hated himself the minute he said it, realized how much he sounded like his own pamphlet. Why was he being so formal with this woman? He felt exactly like the kind of quack and charlatan he'd worked for years trying to prove he wasn't. He hated his life, hated his smile, hated the sound of his own voice.

He tried to shake off these thoughts as he shook Rose's hand across the table, making it a point to look at her eyes instead of her breasts, then left the consultation room, stayed busy for the rest of the day, forgot all about her.

Meantime, he tried not to think about 9 A.M. Thursday, the time she'd scheduled for her examination. He was so busy Wednesday morning he didn't see Rose during her X-ray session with Jean, and when Jean handed him Rose's X-rays that afternoon, he simply marked them with a pencil and a ruler, noting the slight compression of the lower vertebrae, her pelvis's half-inch dip to the left, the angle of the tilt in her hips.

Saying only "Good morning, Mrs. Kindred" when she shook his hand across the consultation table Thursday morning, he went straight to the X-ray light box and pointed to his pencil marks along the spinal column, telling her how the nerves were pinching where her lower vertebrae were compressed, how a slight spinal and hip misalignment and muscle weakness in her lower back and abdomen had caused her severe muscle spasms. If this condition were not corrected, he explained, she could eventually develop a serious degenerative back condition.

"Like this." He clipped another X-ray into the light box to show Rose a severe case he'd worked with last year, a man in his mid-fifties with severe compression in his lower vertebrae, severe degeneration of his spinal discs, and sharp bone spurs growing where vertebrae pressed against vertebrae.

He looked back at Rose sitting at the consultation table. She stretched and popped the silicone nerve roots growing out between the vertebrae on the plastic spinal skeleton. She wasn't paying any attention to what he was saying.

"Mrs. Kindred," he said, "this is important."

"Too much vocabulary for *this* girl." She laughed.

"I'm sorry. I suppose I could be a little more plainspoken."

"No, I'm following you all right, Doc. What's getting to me is this Mrs. Kindred business. Look, as far as I'm concerned, I'm not a goddamn *Mrs.* anymore. I'm sure as hell not any kin to the Kindreds, so don't call me that, okay? I'm just Rose. Till I get my own name back. Just Rose."

He flipped off the switch to the X-ray light box. "All right, Rose, do you have any questions about all this so far?"

She shook her head, chewed her lower lip.

"Then let me take you down the hall for your examination. I still need to fine-tune a diagnosis of your back problems."

In the examination room, he handed her a green open-back hospital gown. "Now, I'm going to step out for a moment while you get undressed. Go ahead and slip this on for me, will you?"

He stepped out into the hall, then over to his office across the hall. A black-and-white poster of giant black ants coming out of a storm sewer, with the headline *Them*, hung over his desk. He checked his watch to see how far behind schedule he was, about twenty minutes, took his schedule book from his desk and checked off the patients he'd seen so far, scratched through three items on his list of things to do, then added an item. The painting subcontractor, who was painting the clinic's sign, had asked that morning if he could abbreviate the sign's letters since the clinic's name was so long: *Southern Illinois Wellness Center.* "Tell painter abbrev okay," he wrote on his to-do list, then put it back on his desk.

He stepped back into the hall and wondered why he'd felt so off balance two days before, why he'd been so worried about this exam with Rose Kindred. True, he hadn't noticed it at first but had to admit it now, Rose was an attractive woman, and her face's slight imperfections actually made her more attractive—the moistness inside the line where her lips met, chapped and frayed where she'd been chewing on them, the tiny >-shaped scar pointing into the corner of her mouth, the brown flecks in her hazel eyes. Her compact dancer's body. Her slender waist. Her wide hips. Her breasts.

She opened the door in the green hospital gown. "All ready for you, Doc." She smiled.

He hesitated at the door, then walked inside, closed the examination door behind him. He took in a breath, let it out.

"What I'm going to do," he said, "is take you through a series of simple tests, first to check your reflex and neural responses, then to check your mobility. Sound all right?"

"Sure thing, Doc."

"All right, then, why don't you sit down here?" He patted the examination table, and Rose sat there. He took her pulse, holding her wrist, looking at his watch as he counted, then picked up his rubber reflex mallet from the exam table, lifted the hem of her gown slightly, and tapped each knee, until both legs made a slight kick. "Well, so far both reflexes and a pulse. Signs of life." It was an old joke, one that wasn't going to work on Rose Kindred. She smoothed the gown back down over her knees.

He reached for a safety pin on the exam table, unclasped it. "Now, I want you to help me here. As I touch you with the point of this pin, I want you to tell me how your legs and feet feel. If you feel a sharpness, say 'Sharp.' If you feel a dullness, say 'Dull.' All right?"

"You ask me, it's all pretty dull." She laughed. "Just kidding, Doc."

Dr. Corley knelt on one knee and took Rose's bare ankle into his hand. He touched the pinpoint against her ankle, then lifted it away.

"Did you feel that?"

She nodded.

"Too much or too little?"

"All right, I guess."

"Just let me know if the pressure's too hard, and remember to tell me dull or sharp."

He began touching the pinpoint along the outside of her right ankle, working his way down to just above the arch of her foot, then back up the other side.

"Sharp," she said. "Sharp. Sharp. Sharp. Dull. Sharp."

"Good," he said. He moved his hand up her leg, touching the pinpoint along the inside of her calf.

"Sharp. Dull. Sharp," she said, then, "You know what really pisses me off?"

He stopped. Against his palm, he felt the clean smoothness along the back of her lower calf, the light hair she'd missed shaving inside the curves of her Achilles tendon. He looked up at her face, at her straight blond hair, clipped just below her ears, shaped around her face. Her eyes' flaring pupils reflected the fluorescent lights above.

"Here I am," she said, "my back all out of whack, some man poking me with a goddamn pin, and my old man's probably poking my best friend on some beach in Miami. Makes me mad as hell, you know?"

He didn't know what to say. Why was she telling him these things? Did she tell them to everyone? To the people in line at the Wal-Mart checkout, people with carts filled with tampons and toothpaste and electric drills?

He held her ankle in his palm, looked down to see how beautiful her ankles were, how beautiful her feet, her legs, the delicate veining under her skin, which was the color of eggshells.

He touched her calf again with the point of the safety pin.

"Dull or sharp?" he said.

She wasn't listening. "Know what *else* really pisses me off?" she said.

He shook his head. It was all he could do.

"I miss *her* more than I miss *him*. I'm more *pissed* at her. Isn't that *crazy*?"

She was talking to him, he knew that, but he was looking at the hem of the hospital gown, just below her knees, just at eye level from where he knelt. His hand was sweating against her calf.

"And I'm *really* pissed at her," she kept on. "I mean, I was unhappy and she was unhappy and I told her things about my old man, things she used to get to him because *he* was unhappy. Things she used *against* me. She was my friend, you know?"

"It was a terrible betrayal," he said. His own voice surprised him, how sincere it sounded, how comforting, because he was thinking of something else—pushing the hem of her green gown back over her knees, over her thighs, turning her over onto her stomach, pushing the gown up over her hips.

He stood up, turned his back to Rose Kindred. "My wife," he started to say but stopped himself, then, instead, heard himself say, "I'm sorry those things happened to you." He clasped the safety pin and put it back on the exam table.

There was a long silence, and he felt the same sensation he'd had at the hospital when Trixie's obstetrician had come into the waiting room and told him about the child, when he realized that he was the one who'd have to tell Trixie when she woke up, a woman who'd been so fragile, so afraid of giving birth, that she'd asked for a cesarean, asked to be put under. For a moment he felt the same panic, didn't know where he was. Then he imagined the priest's face, smiling.

"Are we finished?" Rose said behind him.

He went through the motions of scribbling a notation in her folder, felt himself smile, turn around.

"Not quite."

He tried to push away the thought of removing this woman's gown, her bra, her cotton underwear. His left foot trembled in his shoe as it had when Trixie told him that she was leaving with the priest for Minnesota. He shifted his weight to his left foot, which stopped shaking.

"I'd like to test your range of motion first," he said, "and then you can get dressed. Please step over here and stand on these crossed lines."

She stood barefoot where he told her, and he stepped behind her, put his hands on her hips. "Here," he said, "a little to the left," and he helped to line her up over the target on the floor.

He closed his eyes, imagined reaching up to untie the gown at her bare white back.

He opened his eyes, stepped in front of her to check her alignment with the vertical line running up the wall.

"All right, I want you to put your hands on your hips and bend as far to the left as you can go. If it hurts, just tell me. There's no need for you to do this if it hurts."

She put her hands on her hips, then bent over at the waist to the left.

"That's right. Keep both feet planted, and hold that position if you can. Good." He made a notation in Rose's folder. "Now, bend as far to the right as you can."

As she bent right, he found himself watching the movement of her breasts under her gown, looked away, made a notation.

"Good."

"That one really hurt," she said.

"You've got almost no mobility along that side. Did you notice how much farther left you could bend than right?"

She nodded.

"All right, then, just about finished." He stepped next to her, checked her alignment again along the opposite wall. "Now, I want you to bend as far back as you can."

She did as he'd told her.

"Now, bend as far forward as you can. Touch your toes if you can reach them."

"I don't think so." She laughed, bent over.

He saw the crescent of her panty line running over her thighs against the green gown, imagined standing behind her.

"All right, now stand up as straight as you can, shoulders squared."

He stepped behind her, untied her gown strings, opened the gown at the top, laid the strings over her shoulders, where he laid his hands, over her collar bones, on either side of her bare neck.

"What I'm going to do now is try to localize the problem. When I press against your back, just let me know if I'm pressing too hard. And be sure to let me know if you feel any pain at all. All right?"

"I'll let you know," she said, "believe me."

He pressed his thumbs into the soft flesh left and right of her spine, working his way down from her upper back.

"Doing all right?"

"No problem."

He worked his thumbs down either side of the ridges between her vertebrae, into the small of her back.

"Ouch," she said. "There."

"Here?" He pressed with his left thumb.

"Right there."

He closed his eyes, massaged the soft flesh between her left hipbone and her spine, pressing hard to knead the muscles and nerve roots with his fingertips. Then he started to reach up to untie the gown string at her waist, to open the back of her gown at the bottom, imagined putting his hands on her bare hips, moving his hands down.

He stopped himself. Opened his eyes. What in God's name had he been thinking? What had he been about to *do*?

He stepped back, turned around, picked up Rose Kindred's file on the exam table, walked to the door. "All done," he said. "You can get dressed now." He opened the door.

"Hey, Doc?"

He turned around. Rose picked up her blue Wal-Mart smock shirt folded at the end of the examination table, draped it over her arm.

"What's your name?" she said.

"Marshall."

"Is it okay if I call you that?"

"I suppose."

He stepped out into the hall.

"Marshall?"

"Yes," he said.

"Why is it I can't straighten up? I mean, it hurts like hell when I try to straighten up. Feels like somebody's strung me up sideways like a goddamn bow."

"The body can twist itself in terrible ways to regain its natural balance, to protect itself from pain, and in twisting itself can throw itself more off balance, can make the pain even worse." Too formal. He tried again. "In your case, the pinched nerves made your back muscles tighten to protect your back, which pinched the nerves more, which made the muscles tighten more."

He put Rose's folder under his arm, held out his hand to shake hers.

"Go ahead and get Jean to do your therapy for today. Then set up an appointment with Kari for tomorrow, and we'll get you started on your adjustments. We'll also get you working on some exercises to make your back and abdominal muscles stronger, more flexible. You'll be able to straighten out eventually. Right now, though, we just need to stabilize your chronic condition."

Shaking her hand, he smiled, hated himself for smiling.

"Hope you don't mind me unloading on you," she said. "Guess I just don't have anybody to talk to about all this crap, you know? Except maybe my mother, and she's no goddamn help." She laughed. "I'm glad I came here. You're all right for a back-cracker, Marshall. You're an all right guy."

He looked down at his shoes, shifted the folder under his other arm.

"I wonder if you'd say that if you really knew me," he said, felt stupid saying it. Thought, *If you had any idea what I've been thinking, what I was about to do.* He looked back up at Rose, couldn't meet her eyes, and closed the examination room door behind him.

In his office, he stood along his bookshelf wall, staring up at his collection of airbrushed Aurora models on the top shelf: Dracula, Frankenstein, the Wolfman, the Mummy, King Kong, Godzilla, the Creature from the Black Lagoon, the Phantom of the Opera, the Hunchback of Notre Dame.

Of course, he'd heard of cases—dentists, gynecologists, psychologists, chiropractors—who'd crossed the line, but he'd never had any sympathy for them, had nothing but contempt for them, in fact, had never been able to understand how they'd allowed themselves to do it, until he'd almost crossed the line himself. Now, he understood, was angry as hell at himself for having gone so far. *What in God's name is the matter with me?* he thought. *No more.*

He jumped in his shoes when he heard Jean say, "Marshall, here you are," behind him, then turned around and saw Jean tap her wristwatch. "We've got a waiting room full of people, and Jack Polsgrove's been waiting almost an hour."

Next morning, he dreaded getting up, dreaded going to work, dreaded seeing Rose Kindred again.

A little after 9 A.M., running behind again as usual, he found her folder in the chart box outside adjustment room four, hesitated at the door. When he saw her lying face down on the adjustment table, wearing black Spandex bicycle pants and a loose white T-shirt, he looked at her chart immediately, saw the place Rose had circled on the human back schematic, and read her scribbling under the day's entry. He took in a breath.

"Hello, Rose."

She lifted her face from between the padded rollers at the end of the adjustment table, opened her eyes, laid her head sideways on one of the rollers, and put her hair behind her left ear, out of her face.

"Hey, Doc." She stretched, yawned. "Fell asleep. Guess I didn't sleep too good last night."

"Sorry to wake you up," he said. "From your chart, it looks to me like we've not done you much good so far. I think we can do better."

"It's that bitch-from-hell personnel manager, Maureen," she said. "She knows I threw my back out last week, so what does she do? She schedules me to work more hours *this* week."

"If you want me to, I can call her."

"No." She laughed. "*I* can handle the woman."

"I believe you," he said. He put her folder into the chart box on the wall. "Today, we're going to start your adjustments. Afterward, you'll probably feel good for about an hour or two. Then you might feel a little shaky. On your way home, stop off at work and tell Maureen you can't work today, or tomorrow. Then buy a large heating pad. I want you to go home and stay on your back for at least two days. Do nothing else. Alternate between the ice pack and the heating pad, about twenty minutes at a time, and take a break every hour or so. If you start feeling muscle spasms, stay off the heating pad and just use the ice pack. All right?"

"All right, Doc. Marshall, I mean."

"First, I'm going to stretch your lower back muscles, trying to separate the vertebrae slightly to relieve the pinching. Then I'll show you the adjustment procedure."

"You want to know the truth," she said, "this whole thing's got me nervous as hell. I'm mean, here you've got me on the rack, and all. You're not going to break my goddamn back or anything, are you?"

"Not hardly. It's all gentle, painless. Are you ready?"

"Whatever you say."

He walked to the table, laid a strap across the back of Rose's ankles and tightened it, smoothing it across the Velcro strip mounted to the other side of the table. He stepped on the electric foot switch, which raised and lowered the bottom half of the adjustment table, hinging at Rose's waist. Then he pulled out the back of her T-shirt from where she'd tucked it into her Spandex pants, slipped his fingers under her pants' elastic band, and pulled her pants and panties down slightly in the back. He felt along her spine and found the gap between her lowest vertebrae just above her tailbone, pressing up as the table tilted down, releasing the pressure as the table tilted up. He looked up at a watercolor painting of Canada geese flying out over a lake on the opposite wall.

"I hear the Bears trounced the Cowboys last Sunday. Twenty-three to zip." A safe subject, he thought.

"God, don't tell me you're a Bears fan. My old *man's* a goddamn Bears fan."

"Sorry," he said, shook his head, listened to the motor's whir under the adjustment table, tried to think of another topic.

"You know," she said, "the son of a bitch knocked up my girlfriend."

His fingers slipped over her skin, over the ridges of her vertebrae. He repositioned his hand.

"I just found out about it. Another girlfriend of mine told me on the phone last night. The way she'd heard it, they weren't going to Miami Beach at all. They were going to some clinic. To get rid of it. Didn't want to do it around here. Things get around fast around here, you know. Seems like an expensive goddamn trip to get rid of it, though. I mean, they could've driven up to St. Louis. Guess they're having their little vacation now." She laughed.

"Maybe it's not such a good idea for you to tell me these things, Rose. I'm not a marriage counselor. I have no psychological training, you know, so I'm not sure I can really help you."

"I'm just talking. You want me to stop talking, I'll stop."

"No," he said, "it's not that."

She coughed. "What's really hard, you know, is, my old man and me, we were trying to have us a kid. All this time he was seeing her, we were trying. There I was telling her about how hard it was for him and me, and all the time she was doing it with the son of a bitch."

"Rose," he said.

"I'm just glad it didn't happen, you know? Glad I didn't get pregnant. That would've been the worst, when I think about it. But thinking about them together, thinking about him knocking her up instead of me, thinking about them running off to get rid of it, it's real hard to take, you know?"

"It *is* hard," he said. "I know it is. It's terrible."

He hated the sound of his voice, almost a whisper, hated himself. He looked up at the watercolor on the wall, at the Canada geese flying out over the water, pressed against Rose's spine, remembered telling his wife, "We can try again, you know."

She'd been sitting on the bed in the guest bedroom, rocking back and forth, crying, shaking her head.

"No, no, no," she'd said. "Is that *all* you ever think about?"

"A man should be able to sleep with his wife. My God, it's been over two months. And your doctor said you're all right. She said we could try again, said we *should* try again. Besides, all you ever do anymore is cry, sleep half the day. All I ever do anymore is work. There's *got* to be something else. We've got to *try* something else. *Someone* else, anyway, if that's what it takes. This counseling thing at St. James is just making things worse. You know that. It's just not working."

"Not working for *you*, you mean. What about *me*? What if *I* don't want to try again? You're incredibly insensitive, do you know that? You can't *feel* anything. Not for me. Not for anyone. Not even for yourself. Look, if it's not working for you, then *you* try someone else, all right? The hell with you."

He moved his hand up to the next set of vertebrae along Rose Kindred's bare back, pressed up to separate them slightly as the table's end inclined, looked down at her wide hips, at the dimples on either side of her tailbone, looked at her rounded buttocks against her Spandex pants, imagined pulling them down, climbing onto the table, kneeling over her.

He kicked off the foot switch under the adjustment table and remembered the moment his wife told him she wanted to see the priest alone, without him. The Velcro ripped as he pulled the strap from around Rose's ankles.

"I know you probably think I'm some kind of crazy," Rose was saying. "Probably think I hang around with a bunch of crazies."

"No," he said, "I don't think that about you."

"Here lately I've *felt* like I've been going crazy, you know?"

"You're not crazy, Rose. Something bad has happened to you. I imagine it would make anyone feel a little crazy."

He heard his own calm voice, as if he were listening to someone else in the room, talking to her, comforting her, but he was furious with the woman. Why in God's name did she have to tell him all these things? Why couldn't she just keep them to herself? The woman should see a therapist, should go to see a counselor. Then he imagined the priest's face, smiling again, and shook off the image. Thought, *My God, this woman's making* me *crazy*.

Two hours later, a little after noon, he stepped out of the clinic's side exit for a quick lunch at the café across the street, worrying about how quickly he'd gone through Rose's adjustments. Had he been too rough with her? Had he been too rough, too rushed, with *all* his patients since he'd seen her today, since he'd begun seeing her over a week ago? He couldn't remember. Sometimes, he couldn't remember anything, whole sections of his life this last week, this last month, this last year. Then he almost ran into the yellow sign-maker's crane in the parking lot, saw the sign being lowered on a steel cable over his new clinic's mansard roof, saw what the painting subcontractor had painted on the sign: *So Ill Wellness Center*.

"What in God's name have you done?" he asked the subcontractor, who stood next to the crane cab, talking up to the operator.

"What you mean, boss?" The subcontractor scratched the red stubble on his neck.

"Look. Look at the sign. Read it."

"Yeah," the subcontractor said, "so?"

"No," Dr. Corley said, "so *ill*."

"You said I could abbreviate it."

"I don't give a damn what I said. I was wrong. I want it changed. I want the clinic's full name spelled out."

The subcontractor looked over at the crane operator, rolled his eyes at him, looked back at Dr. Corley.

"We'll have to make out a change order, boss. It's going to cost you. About two thousand bucks."

"I don't care."

"All right, then. It's your money." The subcontractor looked up at the crane operator, smiled. "Well, Jerry, looks like we got to put her back on the trailer."

He heard the two men laugh behind him as he walked back up the sidewalk, didn't feel like eating anymore, went back inside the clinic, sat in his office chair.

So ill, he thought—that's how he'd been feeling about himself, about his practice lately. He remembered Rose's examination the day before. Two thousand dollars, that's how much this single distraction had cost him. How many more distractions like this one had he had this week? How much had *they* cost him? How many of his patients were becoming *im*patient with having to sit in the waiting room for thirty or forty minutes, with his being behind, being rushed, with his sloppiness? And then there was what he'd almost done in the examination room.

He picked up his pen, laid his to-do list in front of him, wrote *Rose Kindred* at the top of the list, underlined her name twice.

"Hello, Rose," he said that night on the phone, sitting at the computer desk in his study at home. "I just wanted to check in on you, see how you're doing."

"Oh, hi, Marshall. This is kind of a surprise. Don't get many doctors calling you at home, you know."

"How's your back? Are you staying on the ice pack and heating pad?"

"Haven't done anything *but* that—that and watch game shows all day. Boring as hell, but at least my back muscles aren't jumping around all over the goddamn place anymore."

"That's good. Listen, Rose, I have something I need to discuss with you. Have you got a moment to talk?"

"You got me flat on my back, Doc. I'm not going anywhere."

He hesitated. "Rose, we've run across a bit of a scheduling problem at the new clinic. We're terribly behind all the time, and I was wondering if you'd be interested in a referral to another chiropractic physician?"

"You want me to switch doctors?"

"Exactly. Since you've only been to see us three times, we assumed you'd be one of those most willing to make a move."

"I like you fine, Marshall," Rose said. "I don't know."

He felt terrible. He wasn't helping this woman with his flimsy lie, but he *had* to do something.

"I'd like to refer you to Dr. James Kerr. He's my chiropractor, has been for twenty years. When I found out I had scoliosis as a kid, a severe curvature of the spine, he helped straighten me out, *really* straighten me out, when most of the orthopedists I'd seen had already said I'd be a cripple by the time I was twenty. I trust the man, Rose. I studied in the profession because of him. He's getting up there in age, but he hasn't lost his touch."

"I don't know, Marshall. Truth is, I'd rather stay with you."

"I'd consider it a favor, Rose. It would really help me out."

She paused. "All right, Doc. If it'd help you out. Whatever you say."

He gave Rose Dr. Kerr's phone number and told her that he'd deliver her files to Dr. Kerr personally tomorrow morning, to explain her case. He said good-bye quickly after that, cradled the receiver, then reached across the desk for his list of things to do and crossed *Rose Kindred* off the top of the list.

Now, he thought, he could get some work done.

After eating a TV dinner, he felt a little better, a little less unsettled about the whole Rose Kindred affair. He recorded an "Outer Limits" rerun he hadn't seen since he was a kid. "There's nothing wrong with your television set," the announcer said. "We control the horizontal. We control the vertical." He hit the mute button on the remote control, then went into his study and sat at his desk, typed in a list of his complete Godzilla video collection to update his database on his home computer:

Godzilla	*Godzilla's Revenge*
Godzilla '85	*The Terror of Mechagodzilla*
Godzilla Fantasia	*Godzilla vs. the Sea Monster*
Godzilla Raids Again	*Godzilla vs. Megalon*
Son of Godzilla	*Godzilla vs. Biologica*
King Kong vs. Godzilla	*Godzilla vs. the Smog Monster*
Mothra vs. Godzilla	*Godzilla vs. Mechagodzilla*
Destroy All Monsters	

Lists.

He sat up in his chair and stopped typing at the keyboard when the thought struck him.

For the last eight months, that's all he'd been doing—making lists, long lists of things to do. Lists of groceries to buy. Lists of projects to start. Lists of things he wanted to do before he turned forty. Lists of social events he could go to. Lists of things to tell the accountant, the architect, the contractor, the city zoning board. Lists of things he could do to improve the clinic. Lists of new diagnostic and therapeutic and exercise equipment he could buy. Lists of television shows he could tape. Lists of chores he should do around the house. Lists of things that could fill up his house, his empty house, his empty life.

And now he was making a list of all the lists he'd made.

He looked at the computer screen. Like these other lists, the list he'd been typing into his computer—a list he'd meant to be strictly for fun—had become an empty chore, was damned foolish, when he thought about it. Godzilla movies, for God's sake.

He sat for a long time, twenty or thirty minutes, heard the VCR click off in the living room, then the creaking of the house's wooden beams in the cold attic, felt the full weight of his empty house.

He stood from his chair and walked into the living room, pushed the VCR's eject button, pulled out the "Outer Limits" tape, labeled it, then put it on the bookshelf with the others. He took down the last tape on his computer list, *Destroy All Monsters*, inserted it into the VCR, and turned the TV's volume all the way up.

Then he lay down on the couch across from the TV and tried to think of Rose Kindred's face. For some reason, he couldn't remember much about her, nothing but her laugh, her frankness, her easy cursing. He couldn't understand why remembering her face was so hard. Then it occurred to him that he couldn't remember his wife's face, either, especially since he'd thrown away all her photos eight months ago, all but two or three that also showed his friends or family. And in those photos he'd blotted her face out with a black Marks-a-Lot.

He was surprised how easily he'd forgotten his wife's face.

But the priest, he couldn't forget him, couldn't forget the man's face. Couldn't forget the man sitting in his chair in his church rectory office, legs crossed, hands folded in his lap, smiling at Trixie, who sat across from him on the couch next to Marshall. Couldn't forget the man telling his wife, "The problem here, it seems to me, is that you and your husband both have different ways of grieving. Not incompatible, mind you, just different. You feel your feelings, Trix, while, like too many men, your husband tends to bury his grief in his work, tends to sexualize his pain." The priest averted his eyes from Trixie's at just that moment, had looked down at his hands folded in his lap. But still that smile.

Counselor. Chaplain. Priest. Man of God.

He imagined the priest bending naked over his wife, kneeling behind her and holding her hips, herself naked and kneeling, elbows down on the rectory couch. Then he heard the TV's blaring roar, sat up on his own couch, watched Godzilla rage against the Tokyo night, against the burning city. He picked up the remote control from the coffee table, clicked off the TV, lay back on the couch, closed his eyes.

He was exhausted, exhausted from staying busy all the time, just busy enough to keep pushing away the image of the priest and his wife—his *ex*-wife—together. He felt sick, and he was exhausted.

Then it came to him, Rose Kindred's face, the tiny scar at the corner of her mouth, her brown-flecked hazel eyes, her beautiful ankles. He imagined closing the door to the examination room, kissing her mouth, stepping behind her, untying her green hospital gown, watching it fall away.

He opened his eyes.

How long had it been since he'd thought of a woman in this way? For the last eight months, whenever he'd rented a new release at the video store to watch alone, he'd always fast-forwarded through the love scenes. How long?

Later that night, he lay in the huge king-size bed he and Trixie had bought at Sears only two years ago, just before they'd conceived the child there. He looked up at the dark ceiling, masturbated, felt a release he'd not allowed himself for he couldn't remember how long, felt the shame he'd felt as a boy, an acolyte in a new black cassock, following behind Father Falls—the old priest at St. James Episcopal, dead twenty years now—holding up the cup of hosts, thinking about the roundness of Sherilyn Rossi's breasts under her new ruffled blouse as she bent to kneel at the communion pew, her palms upturned, her mouth open, her eyes closed.

"Hello, Rose," he said two weeks later, standing in the Ten Items or Less line at the Wal-Mart checkout.

"Hey, Doc," she said.

"How's your back?"

"Doc Kerr says I'm going to live." Rose laughed.

"That's good to know. Good to know he's taking good care of you."

She looked down at the checkout conveyor belt, at his empty hands, saw that he had no items to check out, then looked at the line of people that had formed behind him.

"So, Doc, did you forget something?"

"No, I was just wondering," he started. "I was wondering," he said. "I was just wondering if you'd maybe have dinner with me some night this week."

"Me?" she said. "With you?"

"Yes," he said.

"Goddamn." She looked back at the people in line, all of them keeping their eyes on the covers of *TV Guide* and the *National Enquirer* but leaning forward a little to listen. "I don't know, Doc. I guess I'd have to think about that one."

"Go ahead," he said. He waited.

"Excuse me," the woman in line behind him told the man in line behind her, then broke out of line, squeezing past the candy counter. Then the man behind her excused himself, too, and moved over to Register 3. In a moment, no one was in line behind him anymore.

"The thing is, Doc," she began, "my old man, he's been calling me the last week or so, trying to patch things up. My girlfriend, too. Things didn't work out so good for them in Miami."

"I see," he said.

"It's not like anything's going to happen with him and me, you know?"

"Yes," he said. "I understand."

"But—" she started.

"I lied to you about having too many patients, Rose. You should know that. I was attracted to you. I liked your directness. I liked talking to you. I had feelings for you that doctors don't have for their patients, not without trouble anyway. It was my problem, not yours."

She looked at him a while, her mouth open a little. Another line was starting to form behind him.

"Anyway," he said, "I thought I'd try. Rose, you take care of yourself, all right?" Then he was gone.

He started his Escort in the parking lot, put it into reverse, started to let off the clutch, then jumped in his seat when he heard banging on the driver's side window. He rolled his window down. It was Rose Kindred hugging her arms against the cold.

"He's a son of a bitch—did I tell you that? My old man, I mean. I mean, I don't really need all that crap from him anymore, you know?" She stood on her toes, rocked back onto her heels, stood on her toes again. "All right, Doc. Marshall, I mean. I mean, dinner, sure, what the hell." She rubbed her arms, looked back at the store. "I'd better go inside now. They'll fire me for leaving my register, you know? All right?"

"All right," he said.

Three weeks later, she leaned across his couch, kissed him, said, "You're a little uptight sometimes, you know?" They'd been eating pork chops, watching *The Day the Earth Stood Still*.

"Control freak, my sister calls me," Marshall said. "Repressed. Anal retentive. Straight. Got to have all my little ducks in a row, she says." He kissed her. "She's right about some things. I like a straight backbone." He ran his finger down her spine.

Rose shivered a little. "I *like* this sister."

He touched the corner of her mouth. "I like this scar." Then he stood from the couch, took her by the hand and pulled her up, then led her back to his bedroom for the first time.

"I stopped taking the pill a couple months back," she said, sitting on the king-size bed, unbuttoning her Wal-Mart smock shirt. "You know, when my old man and me started trying."

"I have protection," he said, opened his wallet, pulled out the foil packet, held it up. "We should be careful anyway, you know."

"I'd rather not do it tonight, okay, Marshall? I mean, I need a little time, you know?"

"Yes," he said. "We'll wait till we're ready."

"We can do other things," she said and smiled. Laughed.

In an hour, he lay on his side, tracing a circle around her navel. "Last year," he said, "my wife and I had a child." Lying on her back, her head hanging back over the end of the bed, Rose opened her eyes, rested her head on the pillow at the edge of the bed, to look at him. "She was a girl," he said. "It was all very strange, really. My wife, Trixie, was worried all the time, was always holding her stomach, saying, 'What if she isn't perfect?' We knew she was going to be a girl early on because Trixie was always having sonograms done, was always worried about missing toes, hands, ears, eyes. Strange thing was, when she was born, she *was* perfect, a beautiful child really, not all red and crinkled like some babies you see. She was perfect in every way—perfect face, hands, feet, everything—except that she was dead."

"That's terrible," Rose said.

"Yes," he said. "I've had a terrible anger. A terrible hunger." He traced the curve of Rose's left breast with his fingers, cupped her breast in his palm, bent to kiss it.

Then, without knowing why, he wanted to tell her everything—all about his ex-wife and the priest. He started slowly at first, telling her about how his wife stopped talking to him, stopped sleeping with him, after the child died. But when he started in about the priest, the story spilled out of him, and he felt out of control telling it, felt the same rising panic he'd felt the afternoon he'd gone to the church rectory, almost hysterical, telling the *priest* everything—that something terrible was happening to him and his wife, he didn't know what, but he suspected she'd begun seeing someone else, he didn't know *how* he knew, he just knew, and he needed the priest's help, he didn't want to lose her.

"He smiled at me," Marshall told Rose. "He told me to calm down, said I was overreacting. That night, Trixie told me she was leaving me for the son of a bitch. But already I knew. The minute he smiled at me that afternoon, I *knew*. I felt like a fool, a goddamn fool, spilling my guts to the son of a bitch. The goddamn son of a bitch."

Rose smiled, covered her mouth.

He looked at her a long time, heard the sudden quiet, felt the same heaviness in his chest he'd felt after he'd seen the priest smile. He sat at the edge of the bed, picked up his underwear, stepped into it, stood from the bed. Then he reached for Rose's Wal-Mart smock shirt on the nightstand, handed it to her. She held it out in front of her, as if she didn't know what to do with it.

"I can take you home now if you want," he said.

She sat at the end of the bed, her smock shirt in her lap. "Did I do something wrong?"

"I shouldn't've spilled my guts to you like that," he said.

She looked down at her lap, fingered the name tag pinned to her smock shirt's pocket. "No, Doc, I shouldn't've smiled. I just never saw you let *loose* like that, you know? It was funny."

He shook his head. "I'm too goddamn sensitive. Either that or too *in*sensitive. That's what Trixie used to tell me. I don't know what the hell's the matter with me, Rose. I'm just not any good at talking. It's like I don't know how to *feel* anymore, how to *talk* anymore, to you or anybody, without feeling like a goddamn fool."

"Let's check it out," she said, reaching for him. "Come here."

"What?" he said.

"Just come here."

He walked to her at the edge of the bed, and she put her hands on his hips where he stood. Then she unpinned her name tag from the smock shirt in her lap, knelt naked on the floor in front of him.

"What are you doing?" he said.

"Just stand there. And straighten up."

She bent the pin back from her name tag, held her palm behind his calf, then touched his ankle with the point of the pin. She looked up at him and smiled.

"What?" he said.

"Dull or sharp?" she said.

Get
Right
or
Get
Left

Some nights like tonight, when the phone doesn't ring at 3 A.M., I find myself reaching over in my bed for Vickie or under my bed for a quart of Daniel Stewart. When I find both gone, I remember I'm in my wrecked RV with the permanent hookup at the KOA Kampground, and I dress fast in the dark. Sometime after 3:30, I'm driving my Sunbird south from Springdale on Highway 71 toward Fort Smith, past the sign at the foot of Boston Mountain that says *16 PEOPLE KILLED PAST 3 YEARS, DON'T YOU BE NEXT*, then up the skinny road to the top of the mountain, a caravan of big Wal-Mart trucks wedging me to the gravel the whole time, past Our Lady of the Ozarks and the long drop to Clear Creek from Artist Point, then down the backside of the mountain past another sign on

the billboard for the Jesus Name Free Will Baptist Church, which says
GET RIGHT OR GET LEFT.

I try not to pay too much attention to that last sign anymore.
Partly because the Reverend Larry Leehall hasn't changed the plastic
letters this past year since I finally quit Daniel Stewart and Vickie
finally quit me. But mostly because the sign serves to remind me
that Vickie's probably answering the phone on the nightstand right
now, stretching the cord over the bed, and handing the receiver to
my former good bud and business partner, Lloyd Taggart. I look
away from the sign and hold the tight curves, bite off a plug of
Levi-Garrett, and put on a squeaky eight-track tape of Asleep at the
Wheel. Meantime, I keep my eyes out for wrecks, flares, and stranded
drivers.

"Used to do something like this for a living," I tell a Monkey Grip
rubber products salesman from Springfield, Missouri. I turn my Sunbird north again, then watch the steam plume up from the hood of
his station wagon in my rearview mirror. "Was half-owner in my
own wrecker service," I shout at him above the wind coming through
the open windows. "Got used to telling my whole life story to
strangers in the time it took to get from a wreck to a wrecking yard.
Was easier for me stopping drinking than stopping talking." I shake
the salesman's hand before he gets a chance to thank me. "Bucklin
Rudd," I say. "Pleasure's mine. Where you heading before your
water pump seized up?"

"Home," the salesman says, just like it's the last place in the world
he or anybody would ever want to go to. He's got antifreeze spots on
his white shirt and black grease in the hair sticking up behind his bald
spot. He's haggard and pissed, like they usually are.

"Least you got one to go to," I say, then start in on him, like I
usually do.

"How long you been married?" I say. "Twenty-two years," he
tells me. "How many kids?" Three. "How long you been thinking
about leaving?" He just looks at me with a puckered face I've seen a
hundred times that says, *Who the hell are you?* "That long," I say
and take my Razorback Speedway cup from the dashboard to spit.
Then the Monkey Grip salesman looks down the side of the mountain
and says, "How'd you know?"

"Nothing like working half your life for something," I say, "just
to find out you think you're pretty damn sure you don't want it."

"Tell me about it," he says.

So I do.

I start at the part toward the end, sometime after Vickie finally gave up on hiding AA pamphlets all over the house and made up a cot for me in the kitchen so I could answer middle-of-the-night towing calls myself.

There was this call on the kitchen wall phone one night around 1 A.M., I tell the salesman, and the sweet drunken voice of a lady named Ruth Coover on the other end saying, "I hit a loblolly six miles south of Fayetteville, and I'd sure like to keep the police out of this, honey." It was a voice that told me I'd end up blaming Vickie for making me want to tow a woman, drunk and worthless as me, straight to the Motel 6.

Which, of course, is exactly what I did.

Ruth Coover was holding on to the last bit of her good looks about the same way I was holding on to the last bit of my good sense. The desperate way we both went at it in that single bed was proof enough. I took her to be a little younger than me, middle to late forties, and showing it. She had a chipped front tooth and a busted lip from hitting her mouth against the steering wheel of the new Audi her old daddy had bought her. I didn't stop to look so much, I tried to use my imagination a little, and I made it a point to kiss her careful. She turned out to be quick and supple enough to make me forget she wasn't Vickie a few times, and we both stayed drunk enough to keep it from hurting much.

Afterward, when she wasn't passed out, we talked.

"I haven't taken a vacation in seven years," I told Ruth Coover, "and I haven't had a decent night's sleep in twice that long. When the phone rings for a service call in the middle of the night, I'm usually right on the verge of dropping off, but when the phone doesn't ring I swear I can't sleep because I'm too busy waiting for it to. I drink so I can sleep, but my wife makes me sleep in the kitchen and won't let me do it to her when I'm drunk. Which means she won't let me do it to her, period. The whole thing's driving me to cavort with strange women who sideswipe pine trees."

"I'm not a strange woman," Ruth Coover said. "I've just got a few quirks."

"Such as?" I said.

"I'm an addictive personality," she said. "And I tend to leave the men I get involved with because I tend to get involved with the men my old daddy hates. I always leave the scene of the accident. And I'm driving without a license."

"DWIs, I take it," I said. "Never got caught myself. I ought to be a member of the AA Auto Club, not the Triple A. Nobody expects the wrecker driver to be a drunk." I laughed and bent down to kiss Ruth Coover around her fat lip.

I was beginning to like this woman and the whole idea of screwing around. I'd never screwed around before, although I'd tried bragging about it once or twice to people I'd towed who I'd probably never see again, just to see how they'd react. They almost always reacted favorable.

"Let's do this again," I told Ruth Coover. So we did. Then we decided to do it again the next night.

When I showed up early that morning, hung over as usual, at the Rudd and Taggart Full-Service Exxon and Wrecker Service, I told my business partner all about Ruth Coover.

Lloyd Taggart and I'd been buddies a long time. Twenty years or so back, the summer after Lloyd and I'd dropped out of Springdale High, we both picked blueberries, then hauled them to farmers' markets in Texarkana and Shreveport. Made a good living, the two of us, and we were just kids. We had us an old Ford flatbed we both pitched in on, the same flatbed Lloyd welded up into our first tow truck a few years later. All told, we owned three gas stations at different times and gathered up a good fleet of wreckers.

Since that blueberry-hauling business was our first time to go into partnership, I got into the habit of telling Lloyd about first times while we took turns driving south all night long. I told him about the first time Vickie wouldn't go out with me and the first time she finally would, the first time she wouldn't do it with me and the first time she finally did. I told him about the first time she refused to marry me, the first time we fought a few months after we got married, and the first time she got pregnant after trying for a damn long time. Lloyd really liked to hear me tell that last one when I came into work mornings at our first gas station.

Sometimes Vickie got so worked up about having a kid and so worried about not being able to have one, she called me home for lunch and we did it during my lunch hour, or she made me do it before I went on a call at three in the morning, and I'd leave her standing naked on her head with her skinny smooth legs propped up against the wall behind our bed, because she thought that would make a difference, and I'd laugh all the way to a wreck and then when I came back after I towed the wreck in, she made me do it again till dawn and she'd go standing on her head against the wall one more time just to make sure, while I got ready to go to work at the station.

"Bucky," she'd say, standing on her head as I pulled up my trousers, "we still got ten minutes."

Lloyd always liked to hear me tell that one, especially the mornings after bad wrecks. Lloyd and me, we'd spend all night helping the medics cut some dead man out of his Volkswagen, and next morning Lloyd would say, "Tell it to me again, Buck. Just *tell* it." So I did, even after Vickie'd miscarried the first time. And the second time and the third.

Lloyd always laughed when I told it.

Anyway, this was my first time to screw around on Vickie, so I told Lloyd about the whole thing. He didn't laugh. He flipped off the arc-welder in one of the station's service bays, flipped up his welder's mask, and said, "I figured as much. Vickie called me about four in the morning, wondering where the hell you were. We talked on the phone till sunup."

"Vickie called you?"

Lloyd nodded and turned his head a little to hide the funny smile he had on his face. Then he told me I was crazy.

"Hell," I said, "you do it all the time."

"Hell," he said, "I'm not married to Vickie."

Lloyd wasn't married to anybody. Never had been. After I got ahold of Vickie when we were kids, he always swore that he'd stay a bachelor the rest of his life. For years he hung around the My Pleasure, and for years all these pleasures hung around him. Then he seemed to lose his taste for drinking and carousing around so much, bought himself a new tri-hull bass boat and an electronic depth finder. He'd still drop by the My Pleasure every now and again, because he was a needing man after all, but he once told me, "Buck, it's a lot easier catching beaver at the My Pleasure than catching bass at Beaver Lake." At the time, I thought *he* was crazy.

"You got to understand, Lloyd," I told him the morning after Ruth Coover. "Vickie won't have a damn thing to do with me. I'm way past *What's the deal?* and I'm fast approaching *What the hell?*"

"You're blowing it, Buck," he said. "You're blowing it at home, and you're blowing it here. I can't cover for you anymore."

I asked him if the books were screwed up again. I kept the books every month. Always had.

But Lloyd didn't bother to make any reply. He didn't even look at me. He just flipped the arc-welder back on, flipped his welder's mask back down, and didn't say a word to me the rest of the day.

When I got home that afternoon, Vickie wouldn't talk to me either. Which was unusual.

Over the years, she'd gotten into this habit of shouting long stories at me from our bedroom, so I couldn't understand what she was saying most of the time. I'd have to get up from what I was doing in the garage, walk down the long hall to our bedroom, where Vickie was talking, and say, "Baby, I didn't get a quarter of what you said. Now, start over at the beginning, or wherever you want to start, and tell it to me all the way through." We'd both sit on the bed, and she'd tell me all about what her sister in St. Louis had told her over the phone about her cousin Jake in Poteau, Oklahoma. Sometimes, after that, I'd tell her about what happened with Lloyd and me at the station that day, or about a wrecker call I'd made the night before, or about the squashed-up head of that poor bastard we'd cut out of the Volkswagen, and then she'd start kissing on me without me expecting it, and the story would never get finished.

Other times, when I walked into the bedroom, she'd just say, "I was talking to myself, Bucky." I'd take her to mean she wanted to be left alone, and so I'd leave her to her talking. I'd always stand outside the door and try to listen to what she had to say to herself, feeling like I was missing out on something important. Sometimes all she'd say was "Oh God, Oh God, Oh God," and I'd have to go back to the garage.

Anyway, the afternoon after Ruth Coover, Vickie wouldn't talk to me, not even from our bedroom. And I could tell something was up because she wouldn't even talk to *herself* in our bedroom.

At supper, I finally got around to telling her the lie I'd been conjuring up.

"It was one rough night last night," I said. "Had that call about three and did what I could with a couple other wrecks I spotted in the mountains. One was an International Paper truck that jackknifed.

Had to drive all the way back to Springdale to get the big wrecker. Driver was all right. Busted his lip, is all."

She said, "Come off it, Bucky."

"I would've come home," I said, "but I was late getting to work as it was."

"You could've called, anyway," she said.

I already felt bad about my first lie, but I couldn't help going for my second. "I *did* call, a couple of times, but the phone was busy. Who were you so busy gabbing with till sunup?"

"Nobody," she said. "The phone was ringing off the nightstand, and you weren't in the kitchen, so I took the phone off the hook."

For a second, this look came over Vickie's face like someone had jabbed her in the ribs. Then I saw this smile on her face I'd never seen before, like the one I'd seen on Lloyd's face that same morning. When she smiled, though, she didn't try to hide it like Lloyd did. And she didn't look like anyone I knew. She looked like some woman serving lemon pie at a funeral reception.

She said, "I guess you couldn't get through, could you, Bucky?"

I didn't know what to make of that. That smile and that lie of hers surprised me, and I couldn't think of anything to say to her, not after I remembered what Lloyd had told me, not after her face went blank and she stared at her hands for the rest of supper. I decided an hour later to say Lloyd had told me different, but Vickie was going on about her business, wiping the table and such, like nothing was different at all. Then she started whistling while she did the dishes, like she used to years back. She didn't even drop any hints about TV commercials she'd seen for rehab programs at the Charter Vista hospital. And later on, after she'd gone to bed and I went for the Daniel Stewart under my cot, the bottle was still full. She hadn't poured the whiskey out.

I killed the quart off and thought about waking Vickie up while I sat on the cot in the kitchen, but I still didn't know what to do exactly, or what to tell her, till Ruth Coover called about 2 A.M.

"What you say to taking that vacation you've been missing out on all these years?" Ruth Coover said, as drunk as I was, but a whole lot happier. Her old daddy had an RV dealership in Texarkana, she told me, and she thought she could get me a good deal.

I didn't think about it. I just said, "Sure. Why the hell not?"

After I hung up the kitchen phone, I cheered up some. But I decided if I stuck around very long I'd end up changing my mind, so I wrote a note to Vickie and hung it up with the alternator magnet we had stuck on the refrigerator. The note said, "I'm going somewhere to dry out. I'll be gone as long as I'm gone, so don't worry about me. If you need anything, call Lloyd." That note was my last lie, but it turned out to be true. All I wanted to do was find out about this Ruth Coover, but I didn't take the time to think about what I might lose when the finding out was over.

After writing up that note, I went into our bedroom and loaded up a couple of suitcases. I didn't worry too much about waking Vickie up. She was a sound sleeper. After twenty or so years with me, she'd gotten used to the phone ringing in the middle of the night, and she'd gotten to where she'd never wake up until the phone rang three times. Some nights, when we were still sleeping in the same bed, I wouldn't be able to sleep and so I'd prop my head up with my pillow and wait for a call to come in. When the phone started ringing, I'd sit there and count off the rings—one, two, three. If the phone stopped ringing at three, Vickie kept on sleeping, but if it rang a fourth time, she sat up in the bed, hung her legs over the side, and answered the phone. Every time. Then she'd stretch out the cord and hand the phone over to me.

The phone didn't ring that night, though, at least not while I was home, and Vickie slept right through my packing. I sat on what used to be my side of the bed, and I looked at Vickie for a long time. Even asleep, she didn't look like the woman I'd slept with most of my life. I might've known everything about her, but I didn't know who she was.

So I left.

Two hours later, I was on Highway 71 South, heading to Texarkana with Ruth Coover passed out in the passenger seat of my Sunbird. Asleep, she looked just like a woman I'd slept with just once.

Next morning, I was standing on the show lot for Ark-La-Tex Mobile Home and RV Sales, shaking hands with Ruth Coover's daddy. I could tell the old man hated me from the start, but that seemed to please Ruth, and besides, he wanted to make a fast sale.

In his office, Ruth's daddy said, "You hit my daughter?"

I said, "No, sir," then tried to explain about her hitting a tree and busting her lip.

"That's a goddamn lie," the old man said. "Sign here."

I looked at the loan contract on his desk, and I looked at Ruth Coover through the office window while she paced around the show-room. She looked like she'd paced in that same way, in that same place, before. I wondered if that had anything to do with a man wanting to hit her in the mouth.

"Hold on just a minute," I told Ruth Coover's daddy. I walked out of his office and gripped Ruth by the arm.

"How many times have you done this before?" I said, then let go, seeing my white finger marks go pink on her arm.

"More times than either one of us would want to count," she said. She looked to be relieved that she'd owned up to me. Then she sat down on the floor, like she was tired, or like she was going to cry but would rather just sit down on the floor instead. Then she crossed her legs, looked up at me, and said, "Why don't you just go on home now?"

I thought about that one for a second, and I figured Ruth Coover was probably right. I could go on home. Vickie would still be there for me, and we would talk it out, and I would stop drinking again and get the books straight at work. I wouldn't be drunk when I made wrecker calls anymore, and I wouldn't have to sleep in the kitchen. Vickie wouldn't feel the need to call Lloyd, and Lloyd wouldn't feel the need to make Vickie feel better, or the need to cover for me, or any other need. I could just go on home.

But then I looked down at Ruth Coover sitting cross-legged on the floor, and I saw the place that was scabbing over on her pouty upper lip, and I wanted to kiss the woman for some damn reason I couldn't figure out.

Instead, I just sat down next to her in the middle of the showroom at the Ark-La-Tex Mobile Home and RV Sales and said, "You ever been to Beaver Lake?"

An hour later, Ruth Coover and I were back on 71 in my new RV, this time heading north. Of course, as it turned out, we never made it to Beaver Lake. We didn't even make it as far as Springdale.

Ruth Coover and I stopped at three different liquor stores and pulled over at three different rest stops. We boozed it up big and made up the bunk, then threw off the sheets. By sunset, I was so worn out and drunk and sore and stupid with joy, I let Ruth Coover drive in the mountains.

Just after dark, while I was passed out in the back and while Ruth

Coover was most likely passed out at the wheel up front, my new RV skidded in the gravel at the edge of a switchback, then bumped into a culvert, then swerved into a dry creek-bed, then slammed into a concrete pylon holding up a railroad trestle. When a train rattled over my head sometime after midnight, I woke up with a hangover and a fat lip. Most of my front teeth were gone, and so was Ruth Coover.

About 2 A.M. I climbed up half a mile of rock to get to the road, then walked three miles up the mountain road to find a house and a phone. At least twenty cars passed me, but they didn't do so much as slow down.

When I called Lloyd's number at three, he didn't answer, so I called home. Vickie answered on the fourth ring.

I said, "Is Lloyd there?"

Vickie said, "No."

I said, "Let me talk to him."

She said, "All right."

It took a while for Lloyd to answer, so I had time to think about what to say, but when he got on the phone my mind went blank, so I just said, "Lloyd, you're a son of a bitch."

He said, "I know it, Buck. Where the hell are you?"

I told him I'd had a wreck somewhere between Y-City and Needmore, and I needed his help. I told him the job would take the biggest wrecker we had, the one we used to tow semi-tractor trailers.

He said, "I'm leaving right now."

Next day, Lloyd and I didn't say much to each other because we were too busy working together like we always had. We were both glad for such a big job, the toughest we'd come up against in a long time. We borrowed two more big tow trucks from friends in Mansfield and Fort Smith, then spent the whole morning rigging steel cables and pulleys and diesel winches. Late that afternoon, we pulled the RV out from under the trestle and up the side of the mountain.

That evening, we drove together in the wrecker cab, and I turned down the Stroh's Lloyd pulled from the ice chest and passed my way. He nodded his head and didn't drink his beer either, and for a while we talked about what a good job we'd done on that RV, and we both laughed. Then we both fell quiet, and Lloyd looked into the rearview mirror and said, "Buck, it just happened."

I said, "It always just does."

When I got home Vickie was talking to herself in the bedroom.

Mainly, she talked about Lloyd. I stood outside the door for a long time, trying not to listen, before I got around to knocking. After she opened the door, she said something about how bad my mouth looked, and I said, "I guess you love him."

"I don't know, Bucky," she said. "Let me get you some peroxide."

Then I said, "I just need to get a few things. You still think I got a chance anymore?"

But she just said, "I'll go get you some peroxide, Bucky."

"Is that it?" the Monkey Grip salesman says just before sunup. He looks sleepy, a little disappointed.

"That's about as far as I get sometimes," I say. "Every time I tell it I get a little closer to the end."

"Pretty good story," the salesman says and yawns.

"Been working on it for months," I say, "trying to get it right. You know, trying to get it perfect."

"You're getting close," he says, "pretty close."

Next time I look over to the passenger seat, I see that the Monkey Grip salesman's gone to sleep. After that I just keep quiet and watch the sky go pink.

In Springdale I pull the car over at the One Stop Mart and shake the salesman awake. "I've got somebody I can call to come get your car," I tell him, and he thanks me. Then I get out of my Sunbird, walk to the phone booth next to the highway, and dial the number I've been thinking about calling for a year.

The phone rings three times, but I hang up fast before it rings again, then walk back to the car.

I duck my head in to the passenger window and say, "Can't remember the number."

I open the passenger door, reach across to open the glove box, and watch a pile of blue business cards spill into the salesman's lap. I help him put the cards back, all except one. Then I reach for a pen on the dashboard, scratch through "Bucklin Rudd," and hand the Monkey Grip salesman my old business card.

"Best damn wrecker service in northwest Arkansas," I say. "Maybe you should make the call. Just ask the lady for Lloyd."

Folsom Man

Understand, I was just a kid, eighteen years old, and I didn't think I had a thing to be afraid of, except I'd just bought my first car, a sixty-seven Volkswagen Fastback, and I didn't want to drive to the Rockies alone.

My friend Jerry Beason and I'd been talking about it for years, driving up from Dallas to Red River, then up to Estes Park, following the snow-melt along the spine of the continental divide up to Glacier National, all the way up to Banff and Jasper in Canada, if we had enough money to make it that far. Jerry and I'd hunted for sharks' teeth in the old limestone quarry behind our houses, and we swore we'd become archaeologists and find new dinosaur species out West. Of course, none of it turned out that way. Last I heard, Jerry'd gone into Chapter Eleven trying to sell seismic gear down in Houston. You know the story.

Jerry backed out on me at the last minute, like I knew he would, over some girl he was afraid would dump him if he left. I'd saved close to three hundred dollars and I'd already asked off the whole month of June at the T.G.I. Friday's over on Greenville Avenue, where I'd spent all winter long bussing tables for these pointy-collar Highland Park types my age who went to SMU and listened to the Bee Gees. I had the time off and the money to go, but I was stumped about what to do, and just for the hell of it asked this guy Ned Upson I'd met on a geology field trip over at Eastfield Community College. Part of it was, Upson had a Coleman stove and an old eight-track of *The Who Live at Leeds*. He wasn't exactly a friend.

The whole thirteen-hour trip from Dallas, through Wichita Falls, across the Texas Panhandle, then over through Texline and into New Mexico, Upson said maybe ten words.

"Armadillo," he said, pointing to a road kill on the shoulder, like it was some kind of big revelation to him, or "Pit stop," when he saw a gas station, or "What time you got?" or "Where are we?" like it really mattered when or where. Then he sat back and rocked in the passenger seat, making a spring-squeaking noise that just about drove me out of my mind. Then he leaned his seat back, laid his head back against the headrest, and dropped off to sleep for hours at a time with his mouth wide open. Snored like crazy. Never once offered to spell me.

A loud lightning storm passed fast over us in the middle of the night while I drove through the volcanic cinder-cone valley in northeast New Mexico, past Capulin Mountain and Folsom, then south of Raton Pass to Red River. It was something to see—like driving back through millions of years, long before a single settler or Indian, long even before the Pleistocene, when just a few miles north of there Folsom Man had first chipped flint against the cold, against his own hunger and loneliness and fear—just me and Ned Upson on that thin two-lane and flashes of lightning ripping down through the low clouds, then big drops of rain and little pebbles of hail coming down hard, like hot pumice rocks from an eruption, then the wind shaking that little car of mine, pushing it all over the road like it was nothing at all, and all these extinct volcanoes strobing in and out of the bright booming flashes left and right. And there I was, just a little excited, just a little scared, wanting to say, "Christ, will you look at that," to Jerry Beason or anybody who could appreciate such a fine and awful thing, and there was Upson in the passenger seat next to me, his head back, his mouth open, snoring away through the whole sound and light show.

Next morning, we drove ten thousand feet up Wheeler's Peak and pitched a two-man tent there, the cold smell of spruce and pine, the clean stars and bright moon overhead. It snowed late that night—a wet snow that had melted by noon the next day—and Upson didn't have anything to say about it, wouldn't talk to me no matter what kind of conversation I tried to strike up, and I started thinking maybe he'd be a lot happier just sitting at home watching TV.

Upson and I cut back over to Interstate 25 and drove north through the flat dry plains of southeast Colorado most of the next day, the Rockies' snowcaps hazy and blue far off to the west. Just outside Denver, we passed a hitchhiker with his thumb out on the other side of the interstate, and Upson said, "Messy cans."

I looked over at him and said, "What?" It was the first thing he'd said all day.

"*Mexicans*," he said. "You know, wetbacks."

"Oh," I said, trying to follow his logic. I watched the hitchhiker pass to the left behind us, watched a car pass him going the opposite direction, then watched him drop his hand and turn around to walk the shoulder until another car passed. Not too many cars were driving on the road in either direction, and the sight of the man walking with his head down made me feel miserable and lonely.

Then Upson started in.

"They're taking over, man," he said, "you know?" He went on a while about his grandmother's house in East Dallas, how it wasn't safe for her to go out now that *they*—Mexicans, I had to guess—had taken over her neighborhood. It was the most I'd heard Upson say in two days, more than I ever wanted to hear him say again.

On the north side of Denver, I saw a Safeway off the interstate. "Guess we'd better stop to get us some groceries," I said. "We got us a long haul." Then I turned right onto the ramp and exited into the Safeway parking lot.

While I pushed the shopping cart around the aisles inside, Upson followed me around, dropping into the cart jars of Jif and Miracle

Whip, bags of Fritos and barbecue potato chips, cartons of orange juice and chocolate milk. Just as the cashier was ringing up the last item from the cart, Upson said, "Listen, man, I'll be right back. I got to call home. Don't want my mom thinking I'm laying out on the road, dead or something."

"Hey," I said, but he was gone.

I was putting the two fat sacks of groceries into the backseat of my Volkswagen, was wondering where the hell Upson was, wondering if I'd ever see any money for the groceries I'd just bought, when he came running to my car, weeping like a lost child.

"Man," he said, wiping at his wet face, "you got to take me home."

"What? Why? What for?"

"It's my grandma. She had a bad wreck yesterday. On Central Expressway. They think she's maybe going to die."

I shut the car door and pushed at it a couple of times with my hip to make it latch. I leaned back against the front fender. I took in a breath.

"Wonderful," I said. Then I looked at Upson and said, "Look, I'm sorry."

It didn't take me too long to convince Upson that driving back to Dallas would take us twenty hours, that he couldn't afford to wait that long. And it didn't take him any time to talk me out of most of the money I had left in my wallet for a flight from Stapleton to Love Field. He'd brought along about fifty dollars—something I found out about when we were breaking camp on Wheeler's Peak—and most of that was already gone.

At the airport thirty minutes later, his pack slung over his shoulder, Upson told me, "I'll pay you back, man. Really."

I nodded, knowing I'd never see the money again, and looked up as a 727 screamed over us, then watched Upson run into the terminal. When I saw the groceries I'd just bought in the backseat of my car, I wondered if I should drive back to the Safeway north of town to get my money refunded. Then I wondered why I hadn't thought about that while we were still in the Safeway parking lot, wondered whether I could even get my money back now. I calculated how much I had left in my wallet, about thirty dollars, plus the money I might get back for the groceries, then tried to imagine driving all the way to Canada on that, even to Estes Park, about a hundred miles north.

"Great," I said. "Just great."

Without thinking about it, I got into my car and turned back onto the interstate, this time heading south. I was driving home, I knew it, all the way back to Dallas.

I was angry as hell at myself, too, doing about eighty-five or ninety, and I was scared, really scared, I didn't know why exactly, when I saw the same lone hitchhiker Upson and I'd seen earlier that day still thumbing along the shoulder south of Denver. Had something happened to my mother, my father, my kid brother at home? I thought as I passed him. Maybe I should have called home, too. I watched an eighteen-wheeler blow its diesel plume along the other side of the interstate and wondered whether my engine would explode and leave me stranded on the interstate, whether I would die in a head-on with a semi-tractor trailer before I ever got home. Then I looked up into the rearview mirror and saw the hitchhiker far off behind me, his thumb still out.

"Stupid goddamn Mexican," I shouted into the wind.

Then I slowed down. Pulled over.

It took a long time for him to get to my car. He was a long ways behind me, but he'd seen me pull over. He didn't run to the car. He walked.

When he looked at me from the other side of the passenger window, my first thought was to pull off. One side of his face was swollen, distorted, the skin over his cheekbone bruised blue, and he had an open, weepy cut in the brow over his left eye.

I started to hit the gas. Then I saw that he was just as angry as I was, just as scared, and I reached across the passenger seat to unlock the door.

"Where you headed?" I asked him once we'd gotten back up to sixty. I wasn't going to say anything about his face, that much I'd already decided. I didn't need any more trouble.

He looked over at me.

"Your *destination*?" I pointed to the windshield: *that way*.

He turned his bruised face forward to the road. "Oaxaca. México."

"Where you crossing over? At the border, I mean."

He looked at me again, then back to the road. He thought a moment, said, "El Paso."

"I'm heading that way, but I'm cutting east at Raton. I'll have to let you off at Raton, okay? *Comprende?*"

He looked at me again, but I wasn't sure he understood me. He was about my age, maybe a little older, and he wore new Hush Puppy high-tops, new unwashed Levis, and a new blue jean jacket, with the factory creases still in them. There was a rip along the inside seam of his right leg and a raw scraped place on his exposed right knee. He unbuttoned his jacket pocket and pulled out a blue bandana, buttoned the pocket back, then unfolded the bandana and dabbed at the weepy cut over his eye.

I drove a while, and we said nothing more.

"Aren't you hot?" I said after about an hour, wishing I knew a little more Spanish. It was getting to be late afternoon, and we were both sweating pretty good. His window was still up, the hot air was blasting through mine, but there wasn't any circulation in the car. He'd made no move so far to take off his jacket.

He looked at me again, said nothing, dabbed at the cut over his eye.

I fanned my face, then made a cranking motion with my hand and pointed to his window handle.

He rolled his window down.

"Your jacket," I said, then let go of the steering wheel a moment and gripped the air in front of my shirt like I was holding onto lapels. "It's okay to take off your jacket."

He nodded and leaned forward in his seat to pull his jacket off, then folded it in his lap and reached behind him to put it next to the sacks of groceries riding in the backseat.

That's when I saw the black T-shirt he'd been wearing under the jacket. He'd been cooking in it all this time, out of politeness, and it was sweat-soaked, all except for the silk-screened yellow logo on front, which said *The Wh♂*.

I reached across to open the glove box, pulled out two eight-tracks—Upson's *The Who Live at Leeds* and my *Who's Next*—and dropped them both into his lap.

He looked down at the tapes a moment. Then he grinned and held up his right fist. "All *right*, man," he said, and he gave me a brother's handshake.

"You should do something about that cut," I said, shaking his hand, not thinking much about what I was saying. "You should get somebody to look at it."

He kept grinning at me, kept shaking my hand.

I let go and pointed to my left brow, then to his. He stopped smiling and looked out the passenger window. He dabbed at his cut again with his bandana.

"How'd it happen?" I said. "What happened to you?"

He wouldn't look at me, wouldn't say anything, so I just decided to let it go. I kept on driving.

I'd just put down the sunshade against the afternoon brightness over the mountains, was wondering how much farther it was to Raton—another two or three hours, at least—was thinking about the fine company I'd chosen for my famous adventure to the Rockies, was thinking, Great, now I'd done it, I'd picked up a mass murderer and any minute now he was going to cut my throat and steal my car.

Then he looked over at me and said, "Thiefs. They was thiefs."

I looked at him. "Where?"

He thought a moment. "The Greyhound."

The bus station. I asked him a few questions and he tried to answer them, and in a while I'd put his story together.

He was an illegal who'd hitched a thousand miles west across Mexico the summer before, then crossed over the border somewhere near Tijuana in September and followed the lettuce pickers all the way up California until that spring. Just a few days before he'd taken the bus east, over from Nevada, with the three hundred dollars he'd saved to take back home. He had a big family there in Oaxaca—his mother and a houseful of kids, his younger brothers and sisters.

Two days before, outside the Greyhound station in downtown Denver, two white guys had mugged him, had taken his bus ticket, all the new clothes he'd just bought, his new suitcase, the money he'd saved. Then they tried to take his blue jean jacket, but he'd fought them over that. That was how he'd gotten the cut. Then he'd had to hitchhike through Denver, which meant he'd had to walk because I'd been the first and only person to stop all day.

He had his arm out the window while he tried to answer my questions, and he started beating his fist against the roof of my car. When I started imagining big dents up there, I stopped asking.

We were both quiet a while, him dabbing at his eyebrow, till I said, "Look, you don't have to keep doing that. I got some iodine and Band-Aids back there." I looked over my shoulder to the backseat. "They're there, in my pack." He turned in his seat and reached around to pick the pack up for me, then held it in his lap while I unzipped the front pouch. I pulled out my old first-aid kit with all its rusty dents, popped open the lid, and turned my rearview mirror his way so he could work on himself.

When he'd finished putting the iodine and Band-Aid on over his cut, he put the backpack behind his seat and tried to straighten my mirror for me.

I straightened it a little more, framing the road up behind us, and said, "Thanks." Then I looked back at the grocery sacks sitting in the back seat. "Listen, you hungry? You had anything to eat today? Yesterday? The day before?"

He said nothing.

I reached back, riffled inside the grocery bags behind me, and dropped a loaf of bread into his lap.

"Here, make yourself a sandwich. There's some peanut butter back there somewhere. And some chips."

He looked back at the grocery sacks.

"Go ahead." I nodded to the backseat, and he pulled out the Jif and the Fritos.

"There's orange juice in there, too, and some chocolate milk, but it's probably all hot by now. I forgot to get ice for the cooler." I opened my Swiss army knife and handed it to him, watching him spread the peanut butter on the bread in his lap, then wipe the knife with a clean corner of his bandana, then fold the blade and hand the knife back to me. He looked at his sandwich, then back at me.

"Go ahead," I told him. "You don't have to wait on me."

He lifted the sandwich to his mouth but stopped. Then he took Upson's *Live at Leeds* tape from his lap and handed it over to me.

"Hell, almost forgot." I slipped the tape into the deck I'd wired in under the driver's seat, and he took a big bite of his sandwich, pointing his finger up to the ceiling, grinning at me with his mouth full. I cranked up the volume.

For an hour or so, we drove like that, him eating a sandwich, then fixing himself another one and eating that, too, then another, bobbing his head and banging the roof of my car along with Keith Moon's drum parts while I sang "Magic Bus" and "Shaking All Over." When I put on *Who's Next*, he joined in with me, singing "Baba O'Riley" and "Won't Get Fooled Again" in passable English, his mouth full of bread and peanut butter and Fritos and warm orange juice.

Before I knew it, we'd driven through Trinidad, then through Raton Pass, and had crossed over into New Mexico. Sooner than I expected, we were through Raton, coming up to the east 87 turn-off. The sky and the land had all gone the color of salmon.

I pulled over to the shoulder and looked at him.

"Well," I said, "this is it."

He looked at me, opened his door, and stepped out. He pushed the door shut and nodded at me through the open window. Then he turned in front of my car and started walking, his back to me, his arms folded against the cold of the desert dusk.

I started to exit left from the interstate onto the two-lane, then realized he'd forgotten his blue jean jacket. It was folded next to the two sacks of groceries in the backseat. I reached for his jacket, then leaned forward in my seat to take my wallet out from my back pocket. There was a twenty left inside, a ten dollar bill. I started to take out the ten and slip it into the jacket pocket when I saw my gas gauge at E, looked up into the rearview mirror at the Texaco station we'd just passed a thousand yards off the interstate behind my car. I calculated how much gas money I'd need to get home.

"Damn."

I put the ten back into my wallet, put my wallet back into my pocket, and shifted my car into first, letting out the clutch, hearing the gravel pop under the tires along the shoulder, until I'd caught up with him.

He leaned on his elbows against the window frame.

"You forgot this." I handed him his jacket and watched him put it on. Then I reached into the backseat and handed him the two sacks of groceries up through the open window.

It was almost dark by now, the full moon coming up over the purple hills to the right of the interstate. I turned my headlights on and backed up my car, then braked again and turned in my seat to see him facing me in the brightness of my headlights on the shoulder of the road, a bag of groceries in each arm.

Fifteen minutes later, my gas tank full, I turned my car east onto New Mexico 87, and I drove alone, the stars dimming against the bright moon over the gray cinder cones passing me left and right, and for the first time on my trip I wasn't thinking about when my car would break down on that long stretch or what I'd missed not making it north to Banff and Jasper or even how long I might have left to live. Instead, I thought about the storm I'd passed through on the same two-lane a few days before, about the stranger I'd just left standing along the side of the road. Then I imagined a time a million years off when the rain would wash away the dirt covering my fossil bones and his, would expose them all to the same stars, the same bright moon.

Macauley's Thumb

Three months after his wife, Catherine, died while she picked dewberries at dusk, Cal Macauley nailed his own left thumb over the front door of their log cabin, just above the long rows of rattlesnakes he'd nailed on either side of the door all that hot summer, all the snakes pinned just behind their spades' heads, to the left of their spines, to keep them alive and suffering as long as possible, slapping their long bodies and rattle-tails like diamond-backed bull-whips against the chinked logs, while he watched them die slowly, sick and furious with grief.

He'd spent fifteen minutes trying to find his thumb five weeks earlier, his hand wrapped in his own blood-soaked T-shirt, after his Husqvarna chainsaw kicked off a hidden nail in the beam he was cutting through overhead. It had happened in just the same way he'd warned it might to the three or four couples he and Catherine had contracted to build cabins for over the last six years in the Sans Bois Mountains of southeastern Oklahoma. "Don't hold the damn thing over your head," he'd told an accountant from Tulsa, who'd insisted on using a chainsaw himself, but he hadn't heeded his own advice. He was distracted, trying to remember his last argument with Catherine, unable to shake off the thought of how she'd died, of how she'd been taken away from him like *that*, gone, after they'd argued, a silly stupid argument over something so insignificant he couldn't even remember what it was about. And when the chainsaw kicked back, it slipped out of his hand, then caught him where he'd held the grip, cleaving his thumb off raggedly at the joint where his pointing finger and thumb came together in a *V*, throwing the thumb off into the woodpile behind their cabin. He was ten feet away from the woodpile when he stopped looking for his thumb fifteen minutes later, more afraid of passing out and bleeding to death looking for it than of what might happen if he didn't find it in time to throw it in a bloody ice bucket and take it with him to the hospital in Wilburton to try to get it sewed back on.

He'd been left-handed until the accident, still barely holding on to whatever dignity he could muster in public shows of sympathy about Catherine's death, at the lumber mill in McAlester, at the feed and seed in Red Oak, after he'd wept and shouted and cursed long hours in the loft of his cabin every night. But after the accident he couldn't hold on to *anything* with his left hand anymore—a spoon or a fork, a pen or a pencil, a coffee cup or a shot glass—and he was worried about losing his grip in other ways. Without his thumb, there was no way to hold on to a hammer, or an ax, so he decided to reteach himself how to split wood right-handed, how to strike a hammerhead against a nail head with his right hand without hitting the fingers on his left, without smashing the skull of a rattlesnake he held there against a cabin log, wriggling under a nail point. He was thinking about how Catherine had died, about how he'd *failed* to, when he was trying to split wood for the winter and smelled something dead, awful, and found the shriveled black thumb wedged between two splintered logs. He picked the rancid thing up with his right hand, held it out at arm's length, and walked to the cabin, nailing through the bone and half-rotted flesh where the black thumbnail had already fallen out weeks before, then stood back to look at his own thumb, dead and detached from him forever, smiling at it with the same feeling of nausea and triumph he'd felt when he found the second rattler, coiled under a flagstone, then nailed it to the cabin wall, next to the first rattler, the one that had killed his wife.

It was just the kind of thing Catherine would do, Macauley thought: reaching for the biggest sweetest berry deep inside a tangled dewberry bush down the dusty logging road from their cabin. She'd been angry at him when she left after supper, after their stupid, forgettable argument over the supper table, but he knew she wouldn't've stayed angry long. She'd made her point, whatever it was, and had probably already let it all go, had probably been thinking instead about a way to transplant the yellow wild roses growing along the roadside into the rich mountain-slope humus behind their back porch without exposing the roses' roots to the air and killing them. Killing things was not something Catherine would tolerate, certainly not the slow, cruel killing of the thirty-four rattlers that hung along the cabin wall, nothing that had a *right* to live, she'd say, not even the pine beetles that rattled under the loose bark of their cabin at night while he and Catherine made love, dripping with sweat in the humid loft heat, shouting each other's names as loud as they wanted to without fear of bothering their nearest neighbor half a mile down the road. And that's just what they would've done, Macauley thought, if they hadn't argued. That's what they would've done anyway, even *after* they'd argued, after she'd come back with a sun hat full of dewberries, to make up. It was her way, to fight hard and fair, not to give in, because she had a right, then to let go. It was one of those things she did much better than he did, one of those hard things she made look easy, maybe the best thing about her, the one thing he'd tried hardest, and failed the most often, to learn from her. It's what she would've done. *If* she'd come back.

At just the moment when she reached for the biggest berry, the rattler uncoiled from inside the bush like a cocked spring, struck at her mouth, its mouth wide against hers, its fangs like two curved, white bone hooks, piercing her upper lip, the snake hanging there, both fangs wedged fast between her gums and teeth, injecting their venom before she ever had a chance to shout his name. And Macauley imagined she did just that, as loud as she could, in the terror of that unimaginable last moment, before she blacked out and fell into the tangle of berries and furry thorned vines.

But he didn't hear her. She was too far down the road, and he was too busy feeling sorry for himself in the cabin they'd built together, wishing he hadn't said whatever he'd said to run her off, wishing she hadn't said whatever she'd said to make him stay in the cabin feeling sorry for himself, where he couldn't hear her shout his name.

And because he was feeling sorry for himself, he'd been too stubborn to go look for her, even after the point when he started to worry, even after it was dark for a good long time. And when he finally did go to look for her, his Coleman lantern too bright in his eyes and hissing in his ears, he lost heart too quickly, allowing his anger at her to grow greater than his concern for her, imagining she was out to spite him for what he'd said, whatever it was, and he turned back up the logging road, to spite her. *The hell with you if you'd run off and make me worry about you like this.*

At that moment, he thought of being alone, free of her, free to do whatever he damn well pleased, leaving his wet socks to hang wrapped and steaming over the bathroom light bulb after he'd been fishing, leaving a black ring around the kitchen sink after he'd changed the oil in the Volkswagen bus, not having to hear her say, *You're not listening to me. All right, then, tell me what I just said.* He went to bed alone in the cabin loft for the first time in years, sprawling in their bed because he *could*, because he didn't have to worry about his weight sagging the mattress in the middle of the bed, didn't have to worry about *her* space and *his* space, didn't have to worry about wrapping himself up in all the sheets, snoring, grinding his teeth in his sleep, keeping her up half the night. Then, in the next moment, lying in the depression at the center of their bed, he felt the full weight of her absence, not the fear of being alone—he'd lived alone and liked it all the years before he'd asked her to dance the first time at the Poteau VFW—but the full recognition that he *wanted* her there, *liked* having her there, liked talking to her in their bed about insignificant things, liked her maybe a little more than he'd managed to love her, always had. Then he thought about her body, about touching and kissing her freckled arms and legs and shoulders and breasts, tasting her musky saltiness, then both of them holding on and holding off, carrying each other into and through those long moments just before.

The thought of her in their bed and not in their bed kept him awake half the night in the dark loft, starting to get up to look for her again, then lying back down, wavering between anger and fear, until he dressed and drove the VW bus up and down the mountain road, his headlights scaring up whippoorwills that nestled their bellies in the road gravel, his tires kicking up rolling dust clouds behind, coating the scrub pines and oaks along the road with a skirt of gray powder. Back at the cabin, he listened the rest of the night above the pine beetles' bark rattle for her sandal soles scuffing the gravel outside their cabin window, then got up from their bed and dressed again at dawn, stumbling a quarter mile down the road on foot, until he reached the dewberry patch on the cliff above Turkey Creek.

The snake was still alive when he found her.

Almost every night since, he sat up in their loft bed alone, unable to shake off the nightmare of it, the rattler writhing in its kiss. Half a week after the funeral, the night of the day he found the second rattler sleeping in the flagstone's noon shadow, he sat bolt upright in their bed—shouting, weeping, cursing—and he dressed quickly, emptying the burlap bag of rooting potatoes Catherine had stored in the cellar, then carrying his Coleman lantern hissing into the dark. The third rattler he found an hour later coiled in the cool night air, warming its belly on the crooked heaving black top at the foot of the mountain. The fourth he found a few nights later at the edge of a green-scummed pond, the biggest rattler he'd ever seen, seven feet at least, its neck bulging, the hinge of its jaw stretched around a bullfrog's hips, back legs jutting out and still kicking, jittering, from the snake's mouth. All of them he stepped on with his boot toe behind their heads, not to crush them but to hold them down while he pinched them below their venom glands, between the index finger and thumb of his left hand, then picked them up and dropped them, whipping, spiraling, into the burlap bag. All of them he nailed up, then stood back and watched for hours as they thrashed their bodies against each other all along the cabin wall.

The tenth or eleventh snake—he'd lost count, becoming more and more forgetful—was the first to bite him, in the soft web of skin stretching between his thumb and forefinger, the same place where the chain blades would shred skin and grind bone weeks later. Swinging upside down, whirling, snapping at him, its tail rattle a dry, blurred buzzing in his right hand, the snake struck his left hand holding the open bag just as he was dropping the snake inside. His hand swelled like a black rubber glove, but he decided against going to the hospital for the antivenin shot. He didn't even bother to cut deep with a razor blade between the two fang holes, to suck and spit out the snake's venom curling into his blood. He decided to let it alone. The snake bite was a gift, he thought, but it wasn't enough to kill him. It only made him sick, laid him up in the loft bed, his hand throbbing, swollen and heavy under the ice pack in his lap, himself sweating, shouting curses at the cicadas' ratcheting against the July night's heat.

Six weeks later, just after Doc McPhee removed the black catgut stitches from the pink flap of skin stretched out over the bone where his thumb knuckle used to be, he found a nest of rattlers—six of them, little ones—under a rock ledge, scooping them up with his right hand by the squirming knotted handful and dropping them all into the bag, getting bit only once on the tip of his little finger, then taking them up to the cabin loft, his eyes a cold blue burning. He shook the bag, beat it against the bedpost, watched the sides of the bag bulge and bump on the bed as the young rattlers struck blindly inside. He took his time taking his boots and cotton socks off, then thrust one bare foot, then the other, into the burlap bag, waiting for the sharp quick strikes—one, then another, then the next—then sticking his right hand inside, then his left. He considered sticking his head into the bag, too, laughed at the thought of it, but decided instead to nail up the last of the snakes he'd found, all six of them, to the cabin wall before his feet were too swollen to step down the loft ladder anymore, his hands and fingers too swollen to hold a hammer, a nail, a snake. Afterward, he puked three times, then blacked out in the cabin's gravel drive. In the spinning nausea just before, he had two visions of Catherine's face: the first one of her slender sunburned cheeks, her thin freckled nose, the light blond hairs growing along her jaws, her delicate chapped lips, smiling; the second one of a swollen blue-black face, head twice its normal size, eyes and nostrils swollen shut, so little resemblance to the woman he'd loved and argued with for the last six years that he'd made the undertaker screw the casket lid shut.

When he came to in a hospital bed in Wilburton, his legs and arms heavy and useless, soggy and spongy with pus, like waterlogged driftwood, he was mad as hell, not just because he'd failed but because he'd picked such a foolish and painful way to fail, and everyone in two or three counties had probably heard all about it by now, always hungry for any news of someone else's misfortune, especially of the sensational brand, like something they'd read about in a drugstore tabloid: *Man, struck mad by grief, nails live snakes to cabin, attempts suicide by snakebite.*

But no one had heard, it turned out. Hank Potter, his neighbor half a mile down the road, had found Macauley in the gravel drive—in a coma, close to dead, his lips sun-blistered, red ants crawling into the corners of his eyes and mouth—and kept it all to himself. So had Doc McPhee, who made it a point not to tell anyone.

"Look at you, Cal," Doc McPhee told him in the hospital room, shaking his head, swabbing Macauley's bare hip with rubbing alcohol, then giving him a hydrocortisone shot. "You want to tell me what you've been doing up there on that mountain? It's way the hell beyond me. I'd like to know."

Macauley said nothing, refused to talk to the staff psychologist Doc McPhee sent twice by his room the next week. Six hours after he checked out of the hospital, he plugged a spotlight into the lighter socket of his VW bus, then set out again at 3 A.M. to look for the glowing red eyes of rattlers as they slithered along the cliff ledges above Turkey Creek.

He found his own reeking dead thumb in the woodpile a week later, nailed it above the cabin's front door, as he would a horseshoe, for luck, for perverse bad luck, the rows of twenty dead rattlers he'd nailed up the month before hanging to the left of the door, some of them with skins only partly shed and curling down like shredded rice paper, as if they'd tried to move on to their next lives but had been cut off somehow and couldn't, never would. The live rattlers hung in rows to the right of the door, their flaring scales stacked in gray-brown diamonds as they flung their bodies against the cabin wall, their black eyes unblinking under horned brows, their pink wet mouths hissing, spitting, their black tongues flicking the air. He stood back, then looked up at the black fly-covered thumb, at the rusty ten-penny nail head mashing the end of the thumb against the pine log.

For a moment—as if the thumb were still a part of him and he'd just struck it by accident with a hammerhead—he felt a phantom pain, a sharpness, then a dull throbbing, like blood pooling, trapped, underneath the thumbnail's tender half-moon. Then, feeling light-headed and sick, he tried again to remember his and Catherine's last argument, tried to tell himself that, if he *could* remember—what it was about, who'd started it, who was to *blame*—he could maybe find a way to let her go. He hadn't been able to *stop* holding on to her, not even now, not when he knew she was gone and he had to let her go, or die.

He looked at the clearing in front of their cabin, at the stack of loblolly logs he and Catherine had felled and bark-stripped the day she died. He remembered watching her that afternoon, his left boot up on one of the logs they'd just felled, occasionally tipping back and drinking from an iced thermos of sweet sun tea.

Then, again, he was watching her: her chainsaw sputtering and whining, as she notched one end of a pine log, making vertical cuts and chipping out the pieces with the nose of her chainsaw, then rocking the whirring chain blades over the soft pine wood, shaving out a wide shallow *U*, then smoothing out the rough spots, her saw grips braced against her locked arms, her head and shoulders back, wood chips flying into her hair and face. He watched her hard squinting expression, her taut bandy shoulders and biceps, where she'd rolled up her short-sleeved T-shirt, her slender waist and tomboy's hips in khaki shorts, her freckled legs. He watched her focused concentration, her delicate control—almost an artist's touch—then looked over at her chainsaw sculptures, standing like totem poles in a circle, like the ones she'd sold at crafts fairs outside Muskogee and Tahlequah and Ft. Smith.

When he looked back at her, she looked up at him and smiled, then cut off the chainsaw, laid it leaning against the felled pine log. Then she pulled her yellow bandana from her back pocket and whipped it unfolded against her thigh, wiping her forehead, then walking to him, her hand out to him. He handed her the thermos, watched her tip it back, drinking, the sweet tea dribbling in rivulets down the corners of her mouth, down her neck, into the sweaty *V* of her T-shirt, down between her freckled breasts. She handed the thermos back to him, wiped her mouth with the back of her hand, then looked at him a long time, sawdust in her eyelashes.

"You're better with a chainsaw than me," he'd told her—the very last thing he could *remember* telling her—and she'd laughed, then said, "I know," and leaned into him, kissing him, her lips salty and chapped, almost healed under the pink flecks of lip balm she always kept in her back pocket.

Remembering her, Macauley looked down at the wide scar on his mutilated left hand where his thumb had been, at the smooth pink stitch-ridges like drips of melted candle wax, and he understood how his way of remembering her showed how much he'd already begun to forget her as she was when she was most fully herself, separate from him—as she was when they argued, when she told him, *You just remember what you want to remember.* And imagining her voice, *hearing* it, he heard her accuse him of having forgotten their last argument together, then understood that he *had* forgotten and would never remember. The memory of the argument that made her leave had left *him*. It was gone and she was gone, and he was here, alive, alone, and already he was beginning to forget her.

Catherine stood in the cabin's open doorway, leaned against the door casing, her arms folded. She looked at the snakes nailed in rows on either side of the cabin door, then said, *Cal, take a look at yourself. Take a look at what you're doing.*

He stooped to pick up the hammer and burlap bag at the cabin doorsteps and walked to the cabin wall, slipped the hammer's steel claws over the rusty nail heads pinning down the rattlesnakes, then pushed up against the hammer handle, leaning into it, hearing the nails creak against the wood as he pulled them out, one by one, the dead snakes falling to his feet like rag strips, the live snakes falling, then curling, knotting, around their wounds. He picked them all up by the tails and dropped them into the potato sack, then pulled out the nail holding his thumb up over the cabin door and dropped the thumb inside, too.

Down the logging road, he stood on the high cliff overlooking the place where thunderstorms had washed out the road in the spring, where he could smell the sickly sweetness of the sycamores leaning out over Turkey Creek below. A meadowlark sang *serene serene* from a black telephone pole. He looked back over his left shoulder at the dewberry patch, then at the bush where he'd found his wife. Then he looked down between his boot toes on the cliff ledge, out over the drop a hundred yards down to the gray, still water among the rocks. He heard a woman's shout far off, then imagined himself stepping out into air. Then, thinking of himself and Catherine rocking together, shouting, from their cabin loft bed, he held the bag out in his right hand, over the cliff ledge, and he let it go.

Other Iowa Short Fiction Award and John Simmons Short Fiction Award Winners

1992
My Body to You, Elizabeth Searle
Judge: James Salter

1992
Imaginary Men, Enid Shomer
Judge: James Salter

1991
The Ant Generator,
Elizabeth Harris
Judge: Marilynne Robinson

1991
Traps, Sondra Spatt Olsen
Judge: Marilynne Robinson

1990
A Hole in the Language,
Marly Swick
Judge: Jayne Anne Phillips

1989
Lent: The Slow Fast,
Starkey Flythe, Jr.
Judge: Gail Godwin

1989
Line of Fall, Miles Wilson
Judge: Gail Godwin

1988
The Long White,
Sharon Dilworth
Judge: Robert Stone

1988
The Venus Tree, Michael Pritchett
Judge: Robert Stone

1987
Fruit of the Month, Abby Frucht
Judge: Alison Lurie

1987
Star Game, Lucia Nevai
Judge: Alison Lurie

1986
Eminent Domain, Dan O'Brien
Judge: Iowa Writers' Workshop

1986
Resurrectionists, Russell Working
Judge: Tobias Wolff

1985
Dancing in the Movies,
Robert Boswell
Judge: Tim O'Brien

1984
Old Wives' Tales, Susan M. Dodd
Judge: Frederick Busch

1983
Heart Failure, Ivy Goodman
Judge: Alice Adams

1982
Shiny Objects, Dianne Benedict
Judge: Raymond Carver

1981
The Phototropic Woman,
Annabel Thomas
Judge: Doris Grumbach

1980
Impossible Appetites,
James Fetler
Judge: Francine du Plessix Gray

1979
Fly Away Home, Mary Hedin
Judge: John Gardner

1978
A Nest of Hooks, Lon Otto
Judge: Stanley Elkin

1977
The Women in the Mirror,
Pat Carr
Judge: Leonard Michaels

1976
The Black Velvet Girl,
C. E. Poverman
Judge: Donald Barthelme

1975
*Harry Belten and the
Mendelssohn Violin Concerto*,
Barry Targan
Judge: George P. Garrett

1974
*After the First Death There Is No
Other*, Natalie L. M. Petesch
Judge: William H. Gass

1973
The Itinerary of Beggars,
H. E. Francis
Judge: John Hawkes

1972
The Burning and Other Stories,
Jack Cady
Judge: Joyce Carol Oates

1971
*Old Morals, Small Continents,
Darker Times*,
Philip F. O'Connor
Judge: George P. Elliott

1970
The Beach Umbrella,
Cyrus Colter
Judges: Vance Bourjaily
and Kurt Vonnegut, Jr.